Priceless Secret

Priceless
Book 2

Roxy Sloane

Roxy Sloane Books

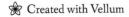

Also by Roxy Sloane:

THE SEDUCTION SERIES:

Priceless: Book Two

Priceless Secret

Vengeance is priceless... Discover the spicy, thrilling new saga from USA Today bestselling author Roxy Sloane!

Revenge. They say it will drive a man out of his mind. But what about a woman? We're supposed to be the fairer sex. Gentle.

Forgiving.

But there's nothing forgiving about the oath I swore: I'm going to destroy Sebastian Wolfe. Even if it costs me everything.

My innocence. My life.

My *heart*.

But what if the line between love and hate breaks forever?

The Priceless Trilogy:

1. Priceless Kiss

2. Priceless Secret

3. Priceless Fate

Sebastian

Everything has a price. Everything, and *everyone*.
Your loyalty. Your morals.
Your love.

At the end of the day, it's all just a transaction, open to the highest bidder. And if you think otherwise...

Well, that just means nobody's offered you a high enough amount just yet.

But believe me, there's a number. A price at which you'll sell your soul to the devil. I've built an empire knowing just what that number will be. When you'll protest, and turn your nose up in righteous indignation.

And when you'll drop to your knees, mouth wet and open for me. Thighs parted, willing to do my bidding.

Ready to scream my name.

And then I met her. Avery. My little sparrow. I bought her fair and square, but it turned out, she wasn't for sale. She cast a spell on me with her innocence and sweet song, fueling my craving for her like nobody else.

With her, it wasn't a transaction, but a *seduction*. Unwrapping the wild heat within her, teasing out her darkest desires, until she was wet and begging for me.

And I took what was mine.

Yes, I was a man possessed. Obsessed.

And I paid the price, alright.

Now I have to know, who is she? What are the secrets she's been hiding from me?

And who will pay the cost of her betrayal?

Chapter 1

Avery

"Let me out of here!" I scream, desperately rattling the doorknob. "Let me go!"

But nobody comes. I've been here for hours, screaming my head off, with no answer.

I'm trapped. A prisoner. And the nightmare is only just beginning.

Stay calm, Avery. There has to be a way out of this.

I pace, trying to control my panic. The last thing I remember is men in medical uniforms dragging me away from Sebastian's house, strapping me into restraints, and sedating me. I woke up, dressed in plain overalls, in a tiny windowless room. The door is locked.

There's no way out.

"Nobody fucks with me. Whoever you really are, you'll rue the day you tried to take me on. No one is coming for you. Your life is in my hands now. And I will get my answers."

Sebastian's final, chilling words echo in my mind.

He's the one who did this to me: Locked me up in a psychiatric facility, supposedly to stop me from harming myself.

It's all lies. I don't know how he pulled it off. Bribed the facility, somehow, to take me away and keep me under lock and key for him. It's barbaric, but then, I always knew he was a heartless monster.

It's why I'm on a mission to destroy him. To crush his heart and ruin everything he cares about—the way he did to me, when he drove the man I loved to suicide.

I thought I was winning. I thought victory was within my grasp. For close to a month now, I've been undercover with him, searching for a way to have my revenge. I created a new identity, new background, played at being sweet and innocent and let him seduce me, all to weaken his defenses and find the best place to strike.

But he wasn't the only one whose defenses were weakened...

I let my guard down, swept up in the heat of our sexual chemistry and the heights of pleasure he drove me to with each new sensual lesson. And when I finally gave myself to him... I thought maybe there was more to the man than just his worst actions, that perhaps, deep down, there was something good there in his soul, too. Capable of love, and tenderness.

How wrong could I be?

Now, I'm trapped here, at his mercy, and for the first time since this dark mission began, I wonder if I'll make it out of this alive.

I tour the room again, searching for anything I missed. It's bleak and institutional: a twin-sized bed, dresser, and a straight-backed chair in the corner. There's an attached bathroom, but it's barely the size of a closet, containing a toilet and sink. There's not even a mirror in there.

Nothing to use as a weapon.

I pound my fist against the metal surface of the door, my face pressed against the plexiglass that allows me to see out in the beige hallway. The fluorescent light outside my cell is flickering ominously, and I feel dread pool in my stomach.

"Let me out of here!" I shout. "I don't belong in here! There's been a mistake!"

There's no one around, but I don't let up. Surely someone has to come?

"I have rights!" I scream. "You can't do this to me!"

But Sebastian has.

I shiver. How could I have been so foolish? I underestimated him.

"Open this door!" I yell, my voice starting to go hoarse and my fist aching.

Finally, I see movement at the other end of the hall. I watch a man in a lab coat walk my way, flanked by two other men in blue scrubs. They're chatting as they stroll along, with no sense of urgency. How can they be so nonchalant while I'm trapped here against my will?

I'm seething by the time the trio reaches my door. I back up as the man in the lab coat unlocks it and consider shoving past him to get out of here, but I know I won't make it far, not with the other two out in the hall.

Talking my way out of this is probably my best option.

"Hello Avery," the one man says as he steps inside the small room. He leaves the door slightly ajar, and I can see the men in scrubs watching me closely, as if I might hurt the guy.

The idea is tempting, to be honest.

"I'm Dr. Reed," he says calmly, pulling the chair closer to the bed and taking a seat. He gestures for me to do the same, but I just cross my arms over my chest and stay in place. Better to be on my feet.

"You need to let me out of here," I say, anger lacing my voice. "I'm not crazy."

"We try not to use that term here; it upsets the patients."

I bite back a bitter laugh. *"That's* what you think upsets the patients? Because I'm pretty sure it's being locked up against their will."

"You won't always be confined to your room, but you need an opportunity to calm down before we can allow you in any of the common areas of the facility." Dr Reed keeps using that calm, smug tone.

I bite back my panic. "You don't understand. I don't belong here at all. This is all because of Sebastian. Whatever he's told you, it's a lie."

Dr Reed gives me a patronizing smile. "Mr. Wolfe is very concerned about you."

I let out a humorless laugh. "Yeah, I bet he is."

"He told all about your erratic behavior, the violence and paranoia. We can help you."

Violence and paranoia? Just what has Sebastian told these people?

"You're not listening," I panic, officially losing all of my patience. "It's all a lie. He wants me to be trapped here... What is this place anyway?"

Dr. Reed gives me a look so filled with sympathy that I want to scream. "You're in Larkspur Psychiatric Facility. We're here to help you."

Larkspur.

Fear chills me. I remember now, the emblem on the van walls.

Oh God. This is the place Sebastian told me about, the one his sister, Scarlett, was trapped after the car accident that killed their father. He described it as hell on earth, he worked for years to get her out of here.

And now, he's trapped me in that same hell.

Monster.

"You can't believe him," I plead. "Listen to me, please!"

The doctor just tuts. "Now, Avery, you need to behave and focus on getting well. I have some medication here that should help with that."

He pulls a pill bottle out of his pocket, and I immediately shake head and back away. "No way. I'm not taking whatever that is."

"It's what's best for you."

"No!"

He turns to look at the men in the hallway and they move into the room without a word. It's a small space, and the four of us take up too much room. Feeling desperate, I try to push by them and out the door now, but it's useless. They grab me firmly and pull me backward, off my feet until my back hits the bed.

Panic claws its way into my blood, making me frantic. I scratch and yell, kicking my feet as much as I can, but they're holding down my legs with strong hands. I'm totally overpowered, I can't take on this many assailants. My eyes lock on Dr. Reed, who has produced a syringe from his pocket. Taking the cap off, he comes close and slides the needle into my arm.

"Mr. Wolfe only wants you to get better," he says, soothing. "We're all here to help you, Avery. Just relax."

I sob, feeling the familiar sluggishness begin to work its way through my system. *Not again....*

Please, no, just listen... I silently beg them.

Then, darkness consumes me.

* * *

When I wake, I immediately know that a lot of time has passed. My body is stiff, and my mouth is dry, like I've been asleep for too long. I groan and try to shift my position on the bed, but I'm restrained. There are thick white straps attaching me to the bed by my wrists and ankles.

Panic rears its head again, but I'm so groggy that it doesn't fully take hold. That should probably be a relief, but I'm too freaked out about the lack of control over my own body to appreciate it. This has to be considered a form of torture.

I look around, seeing that I'm still in the same room. The lights have been dimmed, as if to give me a chance for a peaceful rest.

Yeah right.

"I can see why you're concerned. There are obviously some deep psychological issues at play here."

I turn my head at the sound of Dr. Reed's voice. It's not easy to see from my position on the bed, but I'm able to crane my neck to see that he's standing near the doorway of the room, talking to someone.

"Do you think she'll be okay?"

The other person's voice is tender, but it sends chills through me.

Sebastian.

I strain to see. "The breakdown she had when I suggested medication is a little troubling," the doctor continues. "Our first step here is to make her realize that she needs our help."

Sebastian nods. "I appreciate all your efforts. It feels good to know that she's in the right place. I just want the best for her."

The relieved and wholesome way he's talking turns my stomach. I yank at the restraints, but it does no good.

"Do you mind if I have a moment alone with her?" Sebastian asks.

"Of course. Take as long as you need."

"No," I start to say, but the word is just a harsh whisper because of the sandpaper in my throat.

The doctor leaves, closing the door behind him.

Sebastian slowly turns. My pulse races, taking in the sight of his tall, powerful frame in his immaculately cut suit. His dark hair falls over steely blue eyes that rake over my body from head to toe. I'm trapped here with my captor, already tied down and defenseless, but I know, even if I didn't have a single restraint on my body, Sebastian would be just as commanding.

It's in his blood. His bones. The instinct to dominate surrounds him like an aura.

And God, I submitted to him willingly.

The memories hit me hard, fear mingling with the memory of pleasure in a toxic cocktail as I recall the nights he spent schooling me in seduction, tempting my body with his wicked mouth, and expert hands, and demanding cock, until I was wet and aching for him, caught up in the shameful rush of submission.

He's pushed me to my limits, time and time again. But that was in the service of pleasure.

What does he want from me now?

He stalks toward me, all pretense of gentle concern gone from his eyes. I'm seeing the real man now, and he's cold. *Harsh.*

"Why are you doing this?" I ask, and I'm glad that I don't sound afraid, despite how I feel inside. I don't want him to see my weakness. It's bad enough that I'm in such a vulnerable position.

"You've been lying to me, Avery. If that even is your real name..."

He pulls my necklace out of his jacket, dangling the slim gold chain from his fingertips so that the locket sways, hypnotic. It's just a small, pretty thing, I couldn't bear to part with it. Who knew it would be the undoing of all my careful plans?

I was reckless. Stupid. And now I'm paying the price.

"Because the Avery I thought I knew would have no reason to own this," Sebastian continues, opening the locket to reveal the torn, faded old photo of Miles I keep inside. "No way of knowing this man. So tell me, while you still have the chance: *Who the hell are you?*"

I gulp, my mind racing. I don't know what to tell him.

The truth is out of the question: *'I'm the woman who loved Miles, the good man you embroiled in your gambling circle until he ran up so many debts, he killed himself for the shame of it all.'*

No. If I come clean now about my secret agenda, then it's all over. All my work to avenge Miles' death, the sacrifices and price I've paid to get this close to him will be gone, up in smoke.

Surely, it can't all be for nothing.

I swore revenge. I won't give up now, no matter how bleak it looks.

Somehow, I'll find a way.

"You know who I am," I tell Sebastian, my voice dry and pitiful. "I don't understand why you're doing this to me."

Sebastian suddenly grabs the chair and hurls it across the room away from us in rage. I gasp in shock.

"Bullshit!" he roars, and I'm stunned to see emotion break across his handsome face. Betrayal flashes in his eyes, revealing a pain I never expected to see. "I let you in," he says, stabbing a finger towards me. "I opened up. For the first time, *I trusted you...*"

His voice twists, bitter and desperate, and despite everything, I feel an answering ache, deep in my chest.

Regret.

Because despite everything, Sebastian and I are more alike than I ever imagined. There's nobody we can trust. Nobody we can relax, and show our true hearts, not even for a second. And if our situations were reversed... Then you can bet I would have done the exact same thing. He'd be the one strapped to this bed, at my mercy.

I'd be the one demanding answers, filled with fury.

But there's still one important difference between us. I've made myself into this ruthless monster to defeat him.

Sebastian? He made *himself* this way.

He turns away from me, dragging a hand through his hair. He takes a deep breath, regaining his famous icy control. "Whatever the truth is, I'll find it out eventually. Because you're staying here until I do. Enjoy Larkspur, Avery," he adds, heading for the door. "They're very... hospitable. And I've told them you're in need of extra-special care."

My logic slips. Fear strikes through me.

"You can't do this!" I cry, pulling at my restraints until they bite into my skin. I don't care about the pain; I just need to get out of here. "I'm a *person!* You can't just lock me away like this. It's wrong, and you know it!"

Sebastian glances back. "You should know by now that I don't care about right or wrong," he says coolly. "Winning is all that matters, and believe me, I will be the victor here. Nobody's coming for you, Sparrow. Whatever games you've been playing... They're over now. You're at my mercy now."

He walks out, and the door slams behind him.

"No! Get back here! You can't leave me!"

I keep screaming after him. I can't help it. I've never felt this kind of terror and helplessness before, soon I lose track of my words, lose track of everything except the whirlwind of fear raging all around me, consuming me.

"Nobody's coming for you...."

His chilling words are true. I'm undercover, nobody knows where I am—or how to reach me. I've been communicating with my friends via burner phones I dispose of every time, and they won't think twice if they don't hear from me for weeks—or more.

I'm totally alone.

His prisoner.

Only Sebastian can release me from this nightmare now. And he's just made it clear, he's willing to put me through any hell to get the truth from me. I've betrayed him.

And worse still, I've *hurt him*, too.

That's the shocking truth I saw in his eyes just now. The man who never cared for anything, actually cares about my lies.

But that only makes him more dangerous to me. Because if Sebastian Wolfe will crush his enemies for a game, and destroy empires just to win the upper hand, then what will he do to a woman who's managed—against all odds—to win his affection?

I'm about to find out.

Chapter 2

Avery

I thought I knew what I was getting into when I set out to get revenge against Sebastian. I knew it was going to be impossible to get close to the man who was close to nobody, and even harder to pretend that I didn't loathe him for all the damage he'd wrought with his twisted games. But somewhere along the way, the line between hate and desire got blurred. I let myself be seduced by our sexual connection. I told myself that it meant nothing, and I could stay focused on playing my part, but I ended up blinded by pleasure.

I was supposed to use my sexuality to ensnare him, and that ended up being a far more dangerous game than I anticipated.

Now, I'm facing the consequences.

It's been a week since I was admitted to Larkspur, and Sebastian was right about one thing.

It's hell.

I'm treated like an unruly animal here, kept in a sedated blur and shuffled between my room, and the canteen and 'social' areas with the other patients in some kind of twisted routine. It's almost like being back in elementary school—if elementary school came with armed guards and daily drug doses, and mandatory therapy sessions where they try to make me open up about my violent thoughts.

Thoughts that now run through my mind every night, directed at one person only: Sebastian.

At first, I fought the control and routine, but it made no difference: I was just held down and shot up with drugs anytime I didn't cooperate. There are eyes on me at all times, and I know that—thanks to Sebastian—everyone is wary and on the lookout for any misbehavior from me.

It didn't take me long to realize, I need to be smart to get out of this place.

I need to play their game and act like the perfect patient until I find my chance for escape.

And I will escape. Because I'm a fighter. To the bone. Sure, I let myself grow soft, pampered like a princess there in Sebastian's mansion, with my designer shopping sprees and five-star restaurants, but underneath it all, I'm still the Avery Carmichael that grew up tough, who fought for respect from some of the most twisted mafia players in New York.

Who vowed revenge, no matter the cost.

Sebastian Wolfe has no idea who he's fucking with.

So, I've been playing the model patient for them—and it's paid off. They've finally started to mix up my routine, letting me spend 'social time' time outside in the facility's garden in the afternoons. It's nicer than I expected, with pretty shrubs and flowers, and sure, there's a tall metal fence with barbed wire at the top surrounding the space, which makes it considerably less welcoming, but at least they have wooden benches to relax on, and freshly cut grass, which makes a nice change from the smell of antiseptic and despair lingering indoors.

Look at me, seeing the positive in every situation. The thought makes me want to laugh and cry at the same time.

"Avery?"

I turn to see Dr. Reed approaching me. There are several others working here, so I haven't even seen him since the first day I arrived. He has a small smile on his face, the embodiment of friendliness. He wants me to trust him.

And I'm pretty sure there's a syringe in his pocket with my name on it if I don't do what he wants.

I force a soft smile as he approaches. *Behave.*

"How are you feeling today?" the doctor reaches me.

"Just fine," I tell him. "A little better. It's a lovely day."

"I'm glad to hear that. You missed your lunchtime meds," he says, pulling a capsule of pills out of his pocket. I eye them warily. They won't even tell me what they even are, they just tell me to take them every day—and hold me down to forcefully feed them if I dare disagree.

But now, of course, I'm the perfect patient.

"I'm sorry," I say immediately, and hold my hand out. "I must have forgotten."

"Well, it's a good thing we're here to remember for you." Dr. Reed smarms. "Medication is a crucial part of your recovery. When your brain chemistry is out of balance, it makes it so much harder to be yourself."

He hands me the pill case, and a small bottle of water.

I nod, looking sincere. "I just want to get back to normal," I tell him.

I take two pills from the case and put them into my mouth. I'm being watched closely, so I have no choice.

But I'm a woman of many talents, and deception is right at the top of that list. I pretend to have trouble opening the bottle of water, and it's easy for him to believe I'm too weak to manage it. When he does it for me, I use his split second of distraction to move the pills under my tongue without him noticing.

Once I've taken a sip of water, and swallowed, Dr. Reed

gives a pleased nod. "Excellent," he says. "I hope you'll be well enough to join us in group therapy soon. That's the next step in your program."

I nod, too. "I hope so," I reply. "But I'm feeling pretty tired today."

"Of course. This is a long road to mental wellbeing, Avery, but it's great to see you taking the first steps."

He moves on, to speak with another patient, and I wait until he's out of sight before discreetly spitting the pills out into my hand and crushing them into the dirt with my heel.

No more drugs. No more sedation. I need to be clear-headed now.

There's still some time for our garden break, so I take the opportunity to stretch my legs. Being cooped up in that patient room all day is getting to me, and besides, I have another priority for my brief, precious break.

"Jane!" I call, waving to another patient, who's strolling a slow loop of the grounds.

"Hi Avery," she gives me a tired smile. She's in her thirties, the daughter of some snooty aristocratic family who dumped her here after she had a breakdown from her third miscarriage. Apparently, her husband prefers life as an international play-boy, spending all her money, rather than, you know, taking care of his beloved. "How are you doing?"

"You know, I could use a cheeseburger," I quip. "That canteen slop is getting me down."

She smiles. "What I wouldn't do for some chocolate..."

I laugh. "Oh, I forgot, I found another stone for your collection." I pull it from my pocket and hand it over to her.

Jane has been here for six months, and passes the time by collecting all the flat, oval shaped rocks she can find in the garden. There are plenty for her to choose from, but she's quite particular about the shape of the ones she collects.

I guess we all have to spend the time here somehow.

"It's too round," Jane says, tossing the rock away. "But thanks for trying."

"Maybe I'll find a better one tomorrow!" I say brightly. Jane has been here long enough to know everything about the place, and I need that insight if I have any hope of getting out.

We keep strolling, as I take in the view. I'm not being watched as closely, now that they think I'm cooperating, so I scope as much information as I can. There are orderlies stationed out here to supervise, but not many. My real concern are the security guards, positioned at each exit. They're the real bastards—armed with electric pulse tasers, and not afraid to use them. I've already witnessed them roughly subdue distressed patients without a flash of empathy. I don't stand a chance in a physical altercation with any of them.

"Tell me something, Jane," I say, glancing over at her. She's taken a rock out of her own pocket and is rubbing it between her fingers. "How often do the security guards take a break around here?"

"They only do that one at a time, and the head of security fills in when we're outside. No way out there."

"I didn't say I was looking for a way out."

Jane looks over at me and smiles slightly. "You think you're the first person to come to me like this? Everyone wants a way out at first, but it's not that easy."

She's sharp, despite her time here. Or maybe because of it.

I smile, dropping the casual act. "So, security is a no-go? What about the doctors and nurses? Do you know of any weaknesses there?"

Jane shakes her head. "You should just give the treatment a chance. They really do want to help us here."

Sure they do.

My eyes land on a doctor that I haven't seen before, sitting on a bench and munching a sandwich, clearly taking his lunch break. He's middle-aged and balding, but has a softer look to him than the other staff I've met, who could give Nurse Ratched a run for her money. "Who's that guy?"

Jane looks over. "He's new, just started here last month. I hear he's pretty decent. Does art therapy."

Huh. Interesting.

"Thanks," I smile at Jane. "See you tomorrow?"

"Where else am I going to be?" she says wryly.

I stroll slowly back towards the building, fluffing out my hair as I walk. I may not have any makeup or products here, but ever since I decided to get smart, I've been scrupulous about my hygiene and grooming, doing whatever I can with the plain soap and shampoo in the group bathrooms. The plain cotton sweatpants and shirts they have us in are pretty shapeless, but the navy-blue shade has always been my color. And hell, it's not like this place is a beauty pageant. The other women here have more important things to worry about that looking good.

Men can be simple creatures.

I pause by the bench. "Do you mind if I sit here?" I ask, making my voice soft and breathy.

The doctor looks up at me, and chokes on his food in surprise. "Um, yes, sorry. Please, go ahead."

"Thank you." I take a seat beside him. "I'm Avery. Are you new here?"

"I am. Dr. Wheeler," he introduces himself.

"It's nice to meet you," I offer my hand, gentle, and make lingering eye contact as he shakes it.

The man's cheeks flush. He clears his throat. "Nice to meet you, too. Avery..." he repeats, knitting his brow, "You just arrived, isn't that right?"

I nod. "A week ago. It's been... an adjustment."

"I'm sure."

"I know the program is designed to help me," I add quickly, keeping my eyes wide and innocent. "And I'm really grateful to you all. I guess I'm having a hard time getting used to all my restrictions..."

I'm going for vulnerable with the smallest hint of flirting, and this guy eats it up. I can see it in his eyes, and the way he leans towards me.

"That's a shame. I wonder if I can help at all?"

I sigh. "I really miss listening to music," I say, blurting out the first thing that comes to my mind. It doesn't really matter what I say. I'm trying to work an angle here, to form a connection. "I would always have a record on, but I don't have a way to listen to it now. Since I'm not allowed my phone."

"What kind of music do you like?" he smiles.

"Oh, everything," I smile back. "Maybe it's not cool, but I love all the classic oldies. I grew up listening to them with my parents. You know, the Beatles, and the Rolling Stones..."

He chuckles, and is just about to respond, when there's a shrill whistling sound that can be heard all across the garden. I bite back a curse. Time to get back to my room.

Damn it, I didn't get anywhere with this guy yet.

Still, I'm playing at being the good patient, so I immediately bob to my feet. "I better get back now," I say brightly, like I just can't wait to be confined to that depressing cell for the rest of the day. "It was really nice meeting you, Dr. Wheeler!"

"You too, Avery."

I catch his eyes gliding over my body, so I lean over, pretending to refasten the Velcro strips on the ugly shoes they have us wear.

Sure enough, the nice doctor's eyes linger on my cleavage, just visible through the neckline of my polo shirt.

Hello.

I straighten up. "See you soon," I beam, fluttering my

eyelashes. And then I slowly walk away, sure to put a little extra sway in my hips.

It's cheap, but hell, I don't have many options here. I need to work with what I have. Dr Wheeler is the first friendly face I've seen in this whole place since I arrived, and somehow, I have to convince him to help me get out of here.

An hour later, I discover, that might just be easier than I hoped.

"Dinner's up," the orderly calls, not even knocking before he unlocks my room. I don't get up as he deposits a tray, but then he sets something else down, too.

It's a CD player.

I hide my excitement until he leaves the room, then rush over to investigate. It's a decade old and has probably been gathering dust in a supply closet somewhere, but it runs off a battery just fine, and there's a CD inside: the Beatles' *Greatest Hits*.

I sit cross-legged on my stiff bed and eat the bland food I was brought with a smile on my face as I listen to the music. It's not because I particularly care for the soft rock tunes playing through the speaker.

I'm just happy that I've already made an impact on the doctor.

I'm going to get the hell out of here.

* * *

The next day, I manage to fake taking my pills again in the morning, earning me more goodwill among the staff. I'm still stuck in my room, counting down the hours until I can arrange a meeting with Dr. Wheeler again.

Should I request one of his art therapy sessions? Or would that be too much, too soon. No, it would probably draw too much attention, I'm best just waiting until I can 'accidentally' run into him again.

Finally, I'm allowed outside for my break time. I don't have a way to check my reflection, so I can only hope that I look good when I finally step out into the sunlight and scope the gardens for my target.

I spot Dr. Wheeler, sitting on that same bench. He smiles right away as he sees me approaching. "Avery," he says happily.

"Dr. Wheeler. Thank you so much for the music," I say, making sure to flutter my eyelashes a bit.

He looks bashful. "Well, I know that a small thing like that can really help, and I hear that you're cooperating with your treatment now, so I thought you deserved a little treat."

Deserved a little treat. *You fucking power-hungry idiot.*

I bite back the insult. "You asked around about me?" I ask instead, pretending to be shy and flattered.

"Well, I am a doctor here. My interest is a part of my job."

The hell it is. He's interested in a lot more than he should be.

"You know, working with the creative arts has been proven to be very therapeutic," Dr. Wheeler continues, puffing up a little. "It's actually my specialty."

"Really?" I ask, wide-eyed.

"That's right. Art, music, they can help a patient tap into their core trauma," he says, inching a little closer to me. "Perhaps we can arrange a private session, to explore your issues more..."

"That would be amazing," I exclaim. *Creep.* "But... Can you work that out for me? My schedule is pretty restrictive right now."

"I'm sure we can work out something," he says, glancing at my chest again.

"That would be amazing," I sigh. "I'm so grateful, for all

your help. I don't know how I'll ever repay you..." I beam up at him, and I'm sure that I've got him in the palm of my hand—

Then I hear a slow, clapping sound. "What a performance."

It's Sebastian, strolling over with a sneer on his face—and Dr. Reed beside him. Not impressed.

Fuck.

"Howard," Dr. Wheeler says, bobbing to his feet with a guilty look on his face. "I was just speaking about potential therapies—"

"We heard the nature of the conversation," Dr. Reed says dryly.

Sebastian sighs, tutting. "I warned you that she'd try to do this. She's a troubled young woman, she uses sexual manipulation to get what she wants."

"I don't know what you're suggesting," Dr. Wheeler says, sounding indignant.

"Of course you don't," Sebastian says dryly.

"Well, she can *try* to use her feminine wiles all she wants, but it won't work on me." Dr Wheeler insists. "I'm a professional. Highly trained."

Dammit. I can tell by the way he's blustering that he's embarrassed and angry. Instead of writing my ticket out of here, it looks like I just made another enemy.

"This is all a big mistake," I say, trying to keep my innocent act. "I don't know what he's talking about."

But they all ignore me. Dr. Wheeler gives me a glare. "You know, given the severity of this case, and her antisocial tendencies, perhaps advanced therapy is required. Maybe even electroshock."

"Good idea," the other doctor says immediately.

"Whatever it takes to help her," Sebastian agrees, like I'm not even here. "Perhaps you can oversee her care? I've arranged a six-month hold for her here, to really give her the best chance of recovery."

Six. Months.

Fear chills my blood. He can't be serious.

But he is. "I have to go finalize some paperwork, sweetheart," Sebastian says, giving me a look of triumph. "I'm so glad we had this little talk. I'm about to head out on a business trip, so I won't be back to see you for quite some time. But you'll be in good hands with the doctors here," he adds. "I'll stop by your room to say goodbye before I leave."

I head back to my room in a daze. Sebastian's really doing it: Leaving me here for God knows how long, as punishment for my lies and betrayal.

To break me.

And he might succeed, too. Six months...? I can't imagine spending that long locked away with these doctors and drugs. No choice. No escape.

I can't let that happen.

Pacing the length of the small room, I try not to freak out. I don't see a way out of this, not when Sebastian has so much money and power on his side. He can buy anything, even my imprisonment here.

Maybe Nero could stop this. He has resources. As a mob boss, he's the only person I know that's a match for Sebastian. He's bested him before.

But Nero doesn't know I'm here. He's caught up in newlywed bliss, he's probably not even worried that he hasn't heard from me yet.

No, I can't wait for rescue to arrive. I'm truly at Sebastian's mercy.

Unless...

Unless I do something drastic.

My eyes land on the old CD player, sitting on top of the dresser. When I embarked on this mission, at the very start, Nero gave me a warning. A saying.

When you set out for revenge, dig two graves.

Because vengeance isn't made by half-measures. It demands everything we have to give.

So the question facing me now, is just how far am I willing to go to destroy Sebastian?

What will I risk to see him suffer? How much can I sacrifice before I bring justice to Miles' death?

I've already given him my body, my virginity... Already let him see a glimpse of my heart.

And if Sebastian thinks that I'll stop there, that's all I that I have to give...

He's wrong.

He has no idea what I'm capable of.

I stride over to the CD player and open the tray. I pull out the CD inside, and break it, hard against the dresser.

It shatters, leaving a jagged edge.

I take a deep breath. I don't have much time before he'll return to say his goodbyes, to taunt me some more. I have to do this now.

My heart is pounding as I press the makeshift blade to my skin, deep enough to draw blood.

God help me.

I draw it across my wrists and pray.

Chapter 3

Sebastian

"So, she's taking the medication willingly?" I ask as I scrawl my name on the dotted line of the admission documents. With no family to speak of, it was easy enough for me to present myself as Avery's legal guardian—and I knew, the doctors here wouldn't ask questions, as long as I made it worth their while.

"Yes," Dr Reed leans back in his office chair, looking pleased now that I've transferred the massive facility fees into their accounts. "We had some *difficulties* at first, as you warned us we may, but she seems to have accepted her situation, for now, at least."

"And she hasn't said anything about me, or her... issues?" I probe.

Dr Reed gives a slimy chuckle. "Well, of course she's still maintaining her story of being unfairly imprisoned, but the staff here are used to such delusions. They won't pay any attention to her little stories; I'll make sure of it. After all," he adds, meaningfully, "You have been such a generous patron of our facility."

I resist the urge to smash the man's face into his antique desk. Dr. Reed is a sadistic bastard, but he would have to be to run a place like this. He wasn't in charge back when my sister, Scarlett, was locked up here, I made sure everyone responsible for her suffering got exactly what they deserved, but apparently, there's always a supply of morally devoid medical professionals, ready to use their power to keep people locked up against their will.

For a six-figure fee, of course.

"It's been my pleasure," I lie sliding the paperwork back to him. I never thought I'd be signing another check to these people after I finally won my sister's release. Though I have to admit, I'm surprised that Avery is still refusing to break. I thought a couple of days in Larkspur would loosen her tongue for the truth, but she's far more stubborn than I realized.

Or she's telling the truth, and she really is innocent of any great deception...

I push aside the whispers of my conscience and get to my feet. "As I said, I'll be travelling for business for the next while. I expect regular updates on Avery's condition and care."

"Don't worry," Dr. Reed replies immediately, walking me to the door. "She will be under constant supervision. And as for her privileges..." he gives a nasty laugh, "Those are entirely at your discretion. If you like, we can have her confined to her room 24/7, even adjust her diet and bathroom access. Whatever attitude she arrived with, she won't keep it for long. Our staff has ways of *correcting* any rebellious behavior."

Anger surges, hot. In an instant, I have the doctor backed against the wall. "Nobody lays so much as a finger on Avery." I growl, glaring him dead in the eyes. "And if they do, they better be prepared to answer to me. Do you understand?"

"Of course, Mr. Wolfe," Dr Reed grovels. "My mistake, we'll take good care of her."

"You better."

I release him and stride out of the room. *Fuck.* I pause in the hallway, trying to collect myself. Even after everything, my instincts are to protect her.

Even when I'm the one imprisoning her here, against her will.

But what else am I supposed to do? She's lying to me, keeping secrets. I had a suspicion she was holding something back, right from the start, but I pushed the thought aside, too tempted by her innocence.

Too consumed with the primal instinct to possess her completely.

And that obsession only grew stronger, with every passing day. The breathless kisses I won from her sweet mouth, the moans of pleasure I drew from her untutored body, the sight of her sinking to her knees and eagerly taking my cock into her mouth, choking on every inch in her naïve efforts to please me.

To be my good girl.

God, I've closed billion-dollar deals and sent shockwaves through the stock exchanges around the world, but I swear, I've never known a victory as sweet as finally sinking into her slick cunt and claiming her body for my own. Feeling her clench and scream in ecstasy, overcome by the climax only I could provide. I've never felt a power like it—or such a wild rush of release.

A glimpse of the kind of connection I thought was out of reach for a monster like me.

I should have known it was all a lie. But still, when I found that locket among Avery's things, the discovery cut me deeper than I ever imagined possible.

Miles Romano.

He was one of Nero Barretti's men. A useful idiot, I decided, when he showed up at one of my poker nights last year. But he was low-level, just a street lawyer. Certainly not important enough for me to care about. So, I let him play—and build up a massive debt balance. I figured it could be leverage with Nero one day, but still, the figures were hardly worth my attention. I do billion-dollar deals, what's a couple of hundred thousand to me? When I heard that he'd killed himself, I didn't give it much thought. After all, he was a grown man. I never put a gun to his head and made him play. He made his own choices in life—and death.

But now, the man haunts me for one simple reason: What the hell is his connection to Avery?

I have to know the truth about who she is and why she's here. It's consumed my every waking thought, driving me into fierce rages that have sent half my staff quitting, and the other half cowering in fear whenever I walk into the room.

I'm out of control over her, capable of anything. *Everything.* Which is why she's here, under lock and key in Larkspur. I don't trust myself to resist her long enough to learn the truth. I've been in a cunt-struck haze since the day I met her: It's how she's slipped into my house, my life, past all my defenses.

Yes, she's made a mockery of the great untouchable Sebastian Wolfe, alright. And she'll stay behind these walls until she comes clean—and I can show some goddamn self-control around her again.

I stride down the hallway to her room to say my goodbyes. It's locked, of course, and I snap my fingers to bring the orderly from the end of the hallway. "Open it," I demand.

"Yes, sir." He pulls out a keycard, unlocking the door.

I brace myself, wondering how I'll find her. Resigned, or spitting mad? I've learned that she's not nearly as shy and sweet at she first appeared to be, but I like the fire in her eyes as she stands up to me. It makes me want to tame her even more.

I push the door open—

And everything stops.

She's slumped on the floor, in a pool of blood.

Oh God.

Memories crash into my mind, the night I've tried so many times to forget. Blood pooling on the dark ground, my sister's body, unmoving in the moonlight.

My father's eyes, already lifeless and empty.

Your fault. It's always your fault.

The paralysis breaks. I rush over to her body, yelling at the orderly to call 999, and get help. "Avery," I demand, pulling her upright. She's slashed at her wrists, and I strip off my jacket, pressing it to stop the flow. "Avery, talk to me."

But her body is limp. Eyes closed, her face a ghostly pale color. For one horrible moment, I'm terrified that she's already dead. Then I feel it, a pulse.

Faint, but there.

She's still breathing.

The relief is short-lived. As I cradle her body, willing her to survive, the dark, icy truth settles around me again.

I did this. I drove her to this.

I'm the monster. And there can be no forgiveness for my sins.

Chapter 4

Avery

When I wake, I know I'm not in my room at Larkspur before I've even opened my eyes. The bed I'm in is comfortable, luxurious even after the stiff board I've been sleeping on in that place.

Lifting my head, I groggily take in my new surroundings. I'm wearing silk pajamas now, and they feel good against my skin. The bed I'm in is at least queen-sized, made with the softest linens. The furnishing is soft, with pretty artwork on the walls, and even a flat-screen TV in the corner. This place looks like a hotel room, but there's medical equipment next to the bed, and tubes in my arm hooked up to a gently beeping monitor.

My arm...

I sit up slowly, and my head spins. Taking a deep breath, I wait for it to pass before looking down at my wrists. They're both bandaged, and as I flex my fingers, there's a dull ache from my wounds.

It worked.

I feel a flash of relief—and victory. I got out of that place, alive.

Thank God.

The door of the room opens, and a woman walks in with a tray of food in her hands. She's wearing spotless white scrubs and a warm smile.

"Ah, good. I was hoping you'd wake up soon. The doctor said you could at any time."

"W-what?" My mouth is dry, and my brain seems to be moving slowly as I watch the woman place the tray of food on a table beside me. It smells delicious and when she removes the lid, I see that it's fresh vegetables and a chicken pot pie. Much better than the limp cafeteria food I've been fed lately.

"I'm your nurse, dear. I know you must be confused. You've been unconscious for a day, and you lost some blood, so your mind might be a little muddled. Here," she pours a glass of water from the crystal carafe by the bed, and leans over, bringing it gently to my lips so I can take a sip.

I swallow, feeling better. "How much blood?" I venture.

The nurse checks my bandages, then starts to fiddle with the monitor I'm hooked up to that's displaying my vitals. "You needed a transfusion, but you got lucky. The cuts weren't deep. You'll be fine."

I exhale, as she leaves the room.

She's right; I am lucky. I had no way of knowing how deep I was cutting, I just had to make to make sure that it looked convincing. I had to get myself out of that place.

I feel my stomach rumble, so I don't waste time digging in, knowing that I'll need my strength to recover. The food is great, and I devour it in no time at all. The plate is almost clean when a knock sounds at my door.

"Uh, come in," I call out, adjusting to having the choice of saying 'yes' or 'no'. In Larkspur, they just walked in whenever they wanted.

Sebastian walks in.

I take a deep breath, absorbing the sight of him, impeccably tailored as always in a grey suit, his dark hair looking surprisingly disheveled around his face. Despite everything, I feel an ache in my chest, the muscle memory of attraction already branded deep in my bones.

I fight it. I'd hoped that I would have a little more time before I had to face him, but of course he isn't going to give me that.

Sebastian closes the door behind him and stands there for a long moment, just looking at me. He looks more somber than I've ever seen him before, and it makes him seem older.

I take a slow sip of water. I can already sense the balance of power between us is once again delicate, and I don't want to overplay my hand. I definitely won't be the one to speak first.

Finally, he turns and paces over to the window. He looks out for a long moment, and I watch him, wondering what's to come. More threats? Another demand for the truth?

Will he see through my ruse, or does he believe that I tried to hurt myself, for real?

The lies and games between us run so thick now, I can't tell where they end, and the truth begins.

At last, Sebastian turns to face me. His dark eyes meet mine as he curtly utters the two simple words I was never expecting. Not from him.

"I'm sorry."

I blink in surprise.

"For which part, exactly?" I reply. "Committing me to a mental institution against my will? Keeping me captive? Drugging me?"

"What the hell was I supposed to do?" he exclaims. "You

lied to me! All that time we spent together, and you were keeping things from me. Just tell me, Avery," he demands, pacing closer to me. "The things you told me... The nights we spent together. The way you begged for my cock. Was any of it true, or was it all just a fucking game to you?"

His question echoes in the small room.

That's what he wants to know?

I see the flash of fierce possession in his eyes. My body tightens in answer, pure instinct as it remembers the way that look would always lead to more: His hands on my body, making me moan, making me *beg*. The thrilling domination of his shocking commands—and the rush of my surrender...

The thick, exquisite stretch of his cock driving deep inside me, an ache that's haunted me ever since that night.

I can see it in his eyes, it's haunted him, too. And I realize... It's not over. My plan. My seduction.

My *vendetta*.

Sebastian still wants me. It's so clear in the way he's looking at me. I have a chance to get back in his good graces, if I play my cards right.

If that's what I want.

In a split-second, I make my choice. Or maybe it's no choice at all. After all, I've come this far. Gone to lengths I never imagined possible.

I could never walk away, not until Miles sees justice.

Until I feel Sebastian thrust inside me again...

No. I push that treacherous thought from my mind as I take another breath and drop my eyes, playing with my bandages. Whatever I tell him now needs to allay all his fears. If I'm going to win his trust again, it will take the performance of a lifetime.

I bite my lip and look up at him through my eyelashes.

"Fine," I say, my voice slightly unsteady. "What do you want to know?"

He doesn't hesitate. Walking over to the bed, he pulls my locket out of his pocket and tosses it onto the blanket covering my legs. "What the fuck is this about? How did you know Miles Romano?"

I despise hearing that name come out of his mouth. But I bury that emotion.

"I loved him." It's possibly the first truly honest thing I've ever said to Sebastian. But the rest has to be a lie. I think fast, assembling my story even as his eyes burn into me. "I met him a year ago..." I begin, halting and soft. "After my father died, Nero sent Miles to the farm, to collect what he was owed. But we got to talking..." I swallow. "He was kind to me. A good man. He said he could protect me from Nero," I add, playing into Sebastian's hatred. "He stole away to visit any chance he could. Nobody knew. It was just the two of us, and he promised, he was going to take me away from everything, to give me a better life. Then, he..."

I swallow hard and don't bother to hide the tears in my eyes.

"He killed himself," I say, my voice a harsh whisper. "I didn't even know, until Nero came for me. Miles left me all alone. I had no choices left. That's how I ended up at your poker game."

Sebastian steps closer, gripping my chin to tilt my head back and look into my eyes. "Is that the truth?" he demands, searching my gaze. "No more lies. Because I'm warning you..."

I swallow hard, letting my memories of Miles come to the surface again. This time, to save me. The loss of him aches in my chest. I blink and the tears spill over, rolling down my cheeks.

Genuine. Heartbroken.

"Yes. It's true." I whisper, and Sebastian must recognize the truth in my pain, because he releases me.

I hide my relief, trying to get myself under control again. To game out my next step, while Sebastian paces.

I wipe my tears away. If I was innocent, what would I do now?

"Why are you so mad about all this?" I ask, my voice still thick with emotion. "How did you even know Miles?"

Everything depends on him believing that I don't know what he did to the man I loved.

"I know a lot about the Barretti crime organization," he says evasively, and I can't help noticing that he doesn't hold eye contact. *Guilty bastard.* "Listen, I need to leave today for a business trip."

"Oh. Okay." His sudden change of subject throws me for a loop.

"I will keep it to a few days. The doctor said you can be released this afternoon," he continues, in a clipped voice. "You'll recuperate at my house. I've already hired a nurse for you. You'll have everything you need."

"Will I be your prisoner again?" I ask in a halting voice.

He swallows. "No. That's over. You're free to leave any time you like," he adds. "But for now, you're in no state to travel. I hope you'll wait until I get back."

His eyes meet mine, the question lingering between us.

Finally, I give a halting nod.

He looks relieved. "Focus on your recovery," he says, all business again. "I'll be back in a few days."

He turns walks out of the room, leaving me alone once again.

Chapter 5

Avery

Sebastian's absence makes recovering at his house easy over the next few days. I'm mostly left alone in my suite by Leon and the staff, other than the delivery of three amazing meals a day. The nurse is a friendly, gentle woman who drops by to change my bandages and make sure I'm taking the antibiotics the doctor prescribed, and I have all my clothes and comfy robes, and all the entertainment I could desire.

But it's not a vacation. I have plenty of time to weigh my future.

What the hell am I still doing here?

Sticking around is like playing with fire. He's bought my story for now, but he's also shown me that there's nothing he won't do to those who wrong him. Locking me up in Larkspur is just the tip of the iceberg. I may have managed to get out of that place, but I have the literal scars to show for it now.

What will he do if my story slips again?

I weigh the question for days as I get my strength back and recover. Sebastian swore I wasn't a prisoner, so after a couple of days lazing around the house, I tell Leon I'm taking an afternoon walk, and step out into the fresh air again.

I stroll, taking a meandering path through the neighborhood and nearby park to check that nobody's following me. Then, when I figure I'm all clear, I buy a burner phone at the corner grocery, and call Nero.

He answers on the first ring, and I can hear the concern in his voice.

"Hello?"

"It's me."

He lets out a long sigh. *"Finally. Fuck, Avery. Are you trying to drive me crazy?"*

I can't help thinking about the irony of his word choice, considering where I've been the past week or so.

"Don't worry about me. Everything's fine."

I hate to lie to him, but if he catches wind of what Sebastian did to me, he'll show up to settle things with a .45.

"Are you sure?" Nero asks, low and searching.

"Yeah, it's going so well that he doesn't want to be away from me often. Makes it hard to place a discreet phone call."

I'm getting way too good at lying.

"Well, have you made any progress?" Nero asks.

"I'm not sure." I go back over all the information I've learned about Sebastian and his business dealings, the track I was on before Larkspur cut my investigations short. "He hasn't made any friends with his cutthroat corporate raiding, but the people he screws over are either too destitute or too smart to think about revenge. There are definitely skeletons hidden away somewhere though," I add, strolling, "his family seems pretty fucked-up. After his father died in that car crash when Sebastian was a teenager, his uncle, Richard, took over the company—and married his mom, too. And it turns out, he has a sister stashed away. Scarlett Wolfe isn't dead, after all."

"Interesting."

"I thought so, too." I agree. "She was burned up pretty badly in the accident that killed their dad. It's not much to go on right now, but my instincts say there's something hidden there. I mean, it's one thing for her to want to stay out of the spotlight, after everything she's been through. But why does everyone act like she's dead? I swear, Sebastian never said one word about her before I went and tracked her down."

"Trust your instincts," Nero advises. "Have you dug into the accident yet?"

"No," I reply, frowning. "It was years ago, and Sebastian wasn't even there at the time. You think it's worth looking at?"

"You're the one who said there are skeletons buried somewhere," Nero replies. "If your instincts are telling you something shady is going on..."

"Good point. Where would I even start?"

"There'll be official reports, autopsies, that kind of thing, they won't be hard to access. Trust me, if there's a cop involved, you can pay them off," Nero adds. "You know, I've used an investigator over in Europe before. Charlie's pretty good at digging up dirt. I'll connect you."

"Thanks," I reply, as I hear background voices on his end of the line. Nero covers the phone, his voice turning muffled, and his tone changes, laughing and affectionate.

Lily.

"Listen, uh, I have to go," Nero sounds out of breath, like he's trying not to laugh. Or make some other kind of noise. "Check in soon, OK?"

"Will do."

There's an ache in my chest as I hang up. I would never have guessed Nero could find love and happiness in the midst of his dark, violent world, but Lily came back into his life and proved the both of us wrong. Their partnership isn't exactly traditional, since it started with him forcing her to marry him so she couldn't testify against the Barrettis, but there's no denying the fierce love and loyalty they share now.

It's the kind of love I used to dream about sharing with Miles. The kind of happiness that Sebastian took from me.

I can't let myself forget that.

Yet, when I toss the phone in the garbage and start walking back to Sebastian's place, I realize that my memories of Miles are fading. It's only been a few months since he passed, but a lifetime has happened. Now, the sound of his laugh is an echo of what I used to know, and it's harder to remember the tone of his voice, the expressions that used to be imprinted on my mind.

As if Sebastian has branded his own presence over the top, so sharp and vivid, everything else pales in comparison

Guilt hits me hard.

He's demanding everything from me, but he won't take my memories. No matter how many lies I tell, I know the truth in my heart.

And one day, Sebastian will, too.

When I return to the house, Leon finds me. "Message for you," he says, in his blunt Cockney accent. "And this."

We both look at the tall glass of noxious green liquid that he's holding on a tray.

"Do I want to know?" I ask.

"It's supposed to be good for you," he replies, looking dubious. "Mister Wolfe ordered a whole case of them, all kinds of vitamins and supplements, too."

"I'll stick with your famous vanilla lattes," I tell him brightly. "And the message?"

"Mister Wolfe will be home tonight, in time for dinner. He invites you to join him at eight."

"Invites?" I echo in disbelief. Sebastian doesn't invite, he demands.

Leon gives a small shrug. "I'm just the messenger."

"Thanks." I take a sip of the smoothie and I'm surprised to find, it's not as bad as it looks. I weigh turning down Sebastian's dinner invite, but curiosity gets the better of me. "Tell him that I'll see him then."

I go up to my room to take a long, luxurious shower, nervous anticipation building in my stomach.

Sebastian's back.

The days without him have passed quickly, but his presence has still loomed, full of threat—and temptation. Back at the hospital, he seemed to believe my cover story about how I knew Miles. He asked me to wait for his return before deciding to leave. Now, I wonder if he'll have changed his mind.

What will he want with me now?

The question lingers as I try off, and massage lotion into my skin. The balance of power between us has shifted so many times in the past weeks, it's hard to keep track, but there's one part of our relationship where he's always taken control—and I've loved every minute of it.

Will my sensual lessons with him continue?

My legs spread to his wicked mouth... His hand on my throat as I beg for more... On my knees, serving his cock, desperate for the glow of his praise...

"That's my good little whore."

The memories flash through my mind, and my body comes alive at the thought, shivering and tightening of its own accord. Already wanting him again. My hands glide over my skin, remembering the way he touched me, commanded me, brought me to climax again and again...

I couldn't get enough. It's like he's seen deep into my soul, all the shameful, secret things I've tried to deny.

But there's no denying Sebastian Wolfe. He took every secret desire I couldn't even name and brought them all into the light. Celebrated them. Reveled in them.

Taught me the pleasure of claiming them for myself.

And then there's that night I can't forget, when I gave up my virginity to him. When he took it—and me—with a dark, sensual domination that left me screaming in pleasure, shaken to my core. Needing him in a way I never thought possible, as I gladly surrendered to his masterful commands.

I hate to admit just how many times I've touched myself to that memory, the thick friction of his cock driving deep inside me, filling me so perfectly I could sob for more. Every night, I feel the absence of him, aching and hungry.

And every morning, I wake soaked in guilt, and shame for what my body craves.

Now, there's a mix of anticipation and wariness building in my veins as I dress for dinner. I select a chic black dress with a halter top that ties behind my neck, and a skirt that flows loosely down to my knees. I take time over my hair and makeup. I still have bandages on my wrists from my desperate plot to get out of Larkspur, but I decide to wear them like a badge of honor.

A reminder that no matter how far Sebastian goes to break me, I will always find a way to keep the upper hand.

The clock strikes eight, but I still wait another ten minutes before finally going down to dinner. Sebastian is waiting; he gets to his feet when I enter the room.

"Avery."

His eyes sweep over me, and his lips curl in a familiar

sardonic smile. "You're looking well," he notes, moving to pull out a chair for me. "Your nurse tells me that you're making a full recovery."

Of course, he was checking up on me.

I sit, watching as he pours us both water, and a glass of wine for him. I see no trace of the vulnerability I picked up on at the hospital. The man that apologized to me might as well be gone because he's back to his old self. Completely in control— and infuriatingly sexy.

"I thought we'd give Leon a break, and do takeout tonight," he continues, directing me to the collection of steaming, delicious-smelling containers on the table between us. "Thai is your favorite, isn't it?"

I nod. "Yes."

He doesn't seem concerned by my silence. Sebastian fills a plate for me, chatting about his trip to Brussels, for some finance conference where he gave a keynote speech. "It's a lovely city, but rather quiet," he explains. "They have a lot of art museums, not that I ever have time to check them out. I was in business meetings all week."

I say nothing, slowly taking a few bites of food.

"But it was a worthwhile trip," he continues, casually taking a sip of wine. "The conference is always excellent cover to meet people who might otherwise draw attention, jetting in for a solo meeting. I lined up a number of interesting acquisition prospects."

"How nice for you."

Sebastian glances up at the faint sarcasm in my voice. "Is there a problem?"

I meet his eyes. Even though I'm committed to getting back in Sebastian's good graces, it doesn't make sense for me to just move on like nothing's happened. I've learned he likes it when I push back, and show some fight.

Hell, anyone would make a big deal after what he just put me through.

"Are we really just pretending the last two weeks didn't happen?" I ask, cool.

Sebastian pauses and sets his glass down.

"That's up to you."

I wait, confused.

"What I'd like to offer is a blank slate—for us both," Sebastian continues, serious. He's clearly put a lot of thought into this, and every word is carefully chosen and deliberate. "A chance to start over. Whether you stay or go is your choice now."

"And if I leave..." I sip my wine, studying him.

His jaw flinches with tension, but his voice doesn't waver. "Then I'll offer my assistance. Your debts with Nero Barretti are cleared. You can go back to America, if you wish, or stay in Europe. I'll set you up with an apartment and income, pay for any schooling or business you might enjoy. Or..." Sebastian's gaze meets mine again. "Or you can stay here, with me. Pursue a life here in London. But whatever you choose, it will be just that: your choice. And I will respect the outcome."

I can't believe it. After all Sebastian's twisted games, it feels like a trap, but I see no sign of deception in his face.

I sit back, as if I'm mulling his words. I've already decided to stay and see my vendetta through to the end, but he doesn't know that.

"And what is it *you* want?" I ask, tilting my head.

Sebastian's eyes glide over me. "You know what I want."

My pulse kicks at the sexual suggestion in his gaze. "Why don't you tell me?" I murmur, my voice turning throaty.

Sebastian finishes his wine and slowly gets to his feet.

"I want you," he says, circling the table towards me. "Down

on your knees like a good girl, with that sweet mouth wide open and your cunt slick and ready for my cock."

Oh God.

My thighs clench as his shocking words, my nipples tightening to stiff peaks against the silky fabric of my dress.

Sebastian moves closer, hypnotic. "I want you on your back, tied to my bedposts, kicking and screaming while I gorge my fill of that delicious pussy. I want you facedown, bent over this table with your ass in the air as I fuck you so goddamn deep, you'll feel me for days."

He's standing in front of me now. Tilting my face up to look at him, my body shaking as I'm flooded with a twisted desire for this man.

"I want to own you." Sebastian's voice is thick and raw. His gaze burning into me. "Possess you. Fuck you. Claim you in every way possible, until you can't deny the truth anymore. *You're mine, Sparrow.* And you always will be."

I shudder, filled with a bone-deep ache. I can't remember what my plan was for tonight, or how to handle him anymore. All I feel is this overwhelming need between us, something desperate and dirty and raw.

"I thought you were a man who takes what he wants," I manage, my breath coming fast.

Sebastian's eyes flash darkly, then he's yanking me out of my seat and into his arms. He kisses me hungrily, hard and deep, claiming my mouth with his, thrusting his tongue between my lips as he crushes me closer, and I sink against him, already giddy with the sheer pleasure of his touch.

God, I needed this. Needed *him*. Even as I cursed his name these past weeks, I did it with one hand slipping between my aching thighs to relieve the terrible tension.

Because this is our dance. Hatred warring with passion.

Self-loathing somehow heightening my pleasure. Need over-coming vengeance, just for a little while.

Sebastian tears away, roughly shoving our dinner things aside and setting me down on the table in the middle of the wreckage. He shoves up my skirt and yanks my thighs apart, sounding a low groan as my lacy panties are revealed.

"God, this pussy…" he growls, pressing me back so I'm lying there in the middle of the dinner table, under the grand chandelier. "You could give me every five-star restaurant in the world, but I'd still come back starving for another taste."

Then my panties are gone, and just like that, he buries his face between my legs. *Oh God.* I arch off the table with a gasp of surprise, but Sebastian pins me down, trapping me in place as his tongue laps at me, relentless, spearing inside me then returning to swirl and press at my clit.

"Oh God," I cry out, writhing, shocked by the force of plea-sure that's already surging, cresting inside. I clutch at his head, gasping. "Sebastian!"

"That's right, darling," he growls, thrusting two fingers inside me as my body shakes. "You've been missing me, haven't you?"

I moan, wordless, and he chuckles against me.

"Well, don't worry," he spreads me wider, licks me deeper, "You're going to take my cock so sweetly now. The whole damn city will hear you screaming. And maybe"—he nips my thigh—"if you're a very good girl"—he curls his fingers deep. "I'll bend you over that balcony and let them all watch."

Fuck.

My climax shatters through me in a heady rush, remem-bering the dark of that party, and the eyes on me, watching Sebastian drive me over the edge.

Sebastian's triumphant chuckle brings me back to the

dining room. I lift my head, breathless, to find him watching me, satisfaction written all over his face.

"You think I don't remember?" Sebastian drags me up, even as I'm still shaking with my orgasm. "I know every little thing that gets you wet, Sparrow. Everything you won't even admit to yourself. And I promise, your lessons haven't even started yet."

He half-carries me to the nearest wall. "Palms up," he orders sharply, turning me so my face is pressed against the cool surface.

I obey gladly, body wracked with pleasure—and a sharp craving that I know now will only be satiated by one thing.

Behind me, Sebastian kicks my legs wider, and I hear the metallic clink of his belt as he frees himself. I brace myself, expecting his punishing thrust, but instead, Sebastian pulls my hips back, and sinks into me slowly.

Inch by glorious inch.

His groan sounds, hot against my ear, and I whimper with the feel of him. Pressing against me. Stretching me. Filling me.

Taking me over, until I can't tell where he ends and I begin.

"Avery..." Sebastian's voice is almost pained as he thrusts the final few inches, burying himself to the hilt.

I answer with a sob, flexing around him. He's still uncomfortably thick, stretching me to the limit, but it's a sensation like no other and I sink into the luxurious heat of it all, the weight of his body pressing against me. All I can do is shake with my palms pressed flat against the wall and a crescendo of lust taking me over, his cock impaling me in place.

And then Sebastian eases out, and drives into me again, in one punishing thrust.

I scream.

"That's right, darling," Sebastian fists my hair in his hand, yanking my head back as his hips snap, pounding into me again. "Scream for daddy. Tell the world who owns you."

Fuck. I shudder and moan with the dirty pleasure of his words, but I can't find the answer, not with the thick drive of his cock driving into me, splitting me open, sending me soaring.

"Say it!" Sebastian roars. "Say my name!"

"Sebastian!" I finally cry, as the force of his movements send my body slamming into the wall with every thrust. "Oh God, Sebastian. Don't stop!"

"Never. Fuck, I'm never stopping." He sounds another pained roar behind me, his movements a frenzy now as he claims my body completely. "You don't even know what you do to me. Fuck, even when I hated you, I couldn't stop wanting you. Needing this sweet cunt."

He rips my dress down, squeezing my breast in one hand as the other grips my hip harder, pulling my body back to meet his ravaging thrusts.

"Don't ever lie to me again," he demands harshly.

"Sebastian..." I sob.

"You can't lie. Please, just don't lie..."

There's a strange desperation in his voice now. So I don't. Even in my haze, I obey him. I don't lie, and I swear honesty. I don't pretend my deceit is over, I just chant his name, sobbing as his cock drills deep, and my second climax grows thick in my veins.

"Sebastian! Oh God... *Oh!*"

"*Fuck,* Avery." He comes with a roar, embedding himself deep, and fuck, the feeling sends me hurtling over the edge. I orgasm with him, pleasuring slamming through me in a tidal wave, over and over again until I'm limp and reeling in his arms.

I just hate how it feels like I'm back where I belong.

Chapter 6

Avery

I wish I could say I spent the night awake with shame and regret, but I slept like a baby, alone in my king-sized bed. To my relief, Sebastian seems perfectly happy to keep separate rooms.

It gives me the illusion I still have some boundaries, after he crossed them all so thoroughly—and deliciously—last night. I want to believe that I'm keeping the much-needed emotional distance between us, but in the aftermath of every intimate encounter, I feel like the lines get even more blurred.

Is it worth it?

I take my time in the shower, scrubbing every inch of my body clean that he touched, but still somehow, I feel the burning imprint of his touch.

He's right. I'm going to feel him for days.

When I finally get downstairs, it's mid-morning and Sebastian is nowhere to be seen. I pass the dining room, which has been cleaned, leaving behind no evidence of what happened last night.

If only my conscience was so easy to reset.

I'm just grabbing a bowl of cereal from the kitchen when my phone lights up with a text. Sebastian.

'Tonight?' the message says. *'I'd like you there.'*

There's an invitation attached, to some fancy looking event, celebrating his mother's wedding anniversary... with Richard.

Talk about keeping it in the family. At least she didn't have to change her last name.

'Sure', I text back. The last time I saw Richard at their place in the country, I got some seriously shady vibes. Plus, there seems to be plenty of friction between him and Sebastian.

There's no way I'm missing this opportunity to dig a little deeper into the Wolfe family history.

Sebastian's reply comes immediately. *'Pick you up at 7pm.'*

I tuck my phone away, feeling pleased. My recovery is over, I'm feeling back to my old self again. That means it's time to take my investigations to the next level.

So, I pull my old decoy trip to the spa—having Sebastian's driver drop me at a chic location, then continuing on foot to the branch of the British Library that I've been using for my research activities.

It's been a while since I was here, but the clerk recognizes me as I approach the desk.

"Well, hello there," she smiles. "Back for more? I thought you must have completed your research paper. It's been a couple of weeks since you came in."

"Just a small break," I lie cheerfully. "But I'm ready to get back to it."

The clerk books me into a study carrel and computer, where I can look into the archives. By now, I've gotten pretty good at navigating their system, and I can pick up where I left off with research into Sebastian's business. It's been my primary focus until now because work seems to be the thing that he cares about the most: If I can find a way to hurt him there, it will cut the deepest.

At least, that's what I thought.

But my conversation with Nero is at the forefront of my mind. The car accident, the one that killed his father and injured Scarlett... It was so long ago, Sebastian was just a boy and not even involved, I didn't think it would be relevant.

But now?

I'm willing to try anything.

I put aside my notes about Wolfe Capital and start to search for news reports about the crash, instead. I expect to have to filter through thousands of results, since Patrick Wolfe was already a big deal in the finance world, but as I click through, it looks like there's hardly anything to find, just brief news reports, stating the bare facts. A funeral announcement. A press release about a scholarship fund, established in his name.

That's it?

I open up one of the few newspaper stories I can find.

"Hedge fund wunderkind Patrick Wolfe was killed on Wednesday night when his car lost control and swerved into an oncoming vehicle..."

And that's pretty much it. I frown. Patrick Wolfe was a rich and influential man. His death alone should have made this accident a bigger deal. So, why was it so underreported?

I think about the kind of power and connections that Sebastian has. Connections that could put the lid on a reporter's questions, for sure. But he was a kid back then, just a teenager. He told me himself how he couldn't even get Scarlett out of Larkspur for years.

So maybe it was someone else who kept the press at bay?

Or maybe there's no story here at all, just a tragic accident, like the reports say.

. . .

I spend the next hour scanning anything I can find for additional details, but I don't have any luck. No suspicions of foul play, no signs Patrick was drinking... I can't even find any names for the people in the other vehicle, and there's not even a mention of them in half the articles, so I have to guess that they were all OK.

So much for a fresh new lead. This seems like a dead-end.

I figure I should hit the boutiques before heading back to the house, especially if I have a fancy event to attend with Sebastian tonight, so I pack up and call it a day. I'm just walking out, when I see a familiar face: James. He's pacing in the doorway, talking on his cellphone, but he waves when he sees me, and gestures for me to wait.

I pause, uncertain. The last time I talked to James, someone took incriminating photos of us together and sent them to me at the house as a threat.

But I dealt with Becca. She's probably too busy defending herself against the embezzlement charges I engineered to care about putting a wedge between me and Sebastian now. Besides, James reminds me of Miles in a way, there's a sweet sincerity about him that's a welcome break from all the cutthroat egos I've met in London.

"Hi," I smile, as he ends his call and strolls over.

"Hey, stranger." He greets me with an easy smile. "I was wondering if I'd see you again. Some of us aren't lucky enough to ever be free of this place," he quips, and I laugh.

"Have you been spending a lot of time at the library, then?"

"Only every day," he gives a dramatic sigh. "Makes me wonder why I didn't pick an easier career. Something fun and simple, like firefighting, or Grizzly bear wrangling."

I laugh again. "But think of all the good you're doing with your...?"

"Post-Doc in Industrial English Labor Practices of the late twentieth century?" James replies.

"Right. Exactly. Just what the world needs, whatever that is," I say, smiling.

He laughs. "Want to tell my mum that? She swears I'm wasting my life with academic research."

"So, another vote for Grizzly-wrangling then?"

"Or the Civil Service." I raise my eyebrows, confused. "Don't ask," he says with another friendly smile. "Hey, I don't suppose you have plans tonight? A group of us are meeting for Trivia Night at the pub, if you want to come join. It should be fun. Dorky, but fun."

I feel an odd pang. It all sounds so... Normal. The kind of thing an ordinary girl my age would be doing on a Friday night: beers, and friends, and trivia.

But my life has never been ordinary.

Even before Sebastian, my Friday nights were liable to take a turn into mafia business, and the only drinks I enjoyed were the ones I served behind the bar of Nero's club, with one hand on the gun I kept under the counter. And now...?

Now, I have an empire to destroy.

"Sounds like fun," I tell him, sincere. "But I have a thing, with my boyfriend."

"Ah yes, the mysterious other half." James doesn't seem phased by my response. "Well, have fun, and if you ever feel like joining, the offer stands. We meet every month, make a night of it. Let me give you my number, in case your schedule frees up." He scribbles it on the bag of a flyer, and hands it to me. "I better get back to work," he says. "See you soon!"

"See you," I agree.

I fold the number, and slip it in my bag, already knowing I

won't be calling him. The girl who would hang out at Trivia Night never existed, and James may be a sweet guy, but he could never understand the dark rage that fills my heart or drives my vendetta.

I'm still playing an act with Sebastian, but there's more truth to it every day than the girl James thinks I am.

I've just stepped out of the building when my phone goes off with a text. It's Sebastian. I freeze in panic, wondering for a moment if he's watching me, but then I check the message.

Running late. Meet you at the party.

I exhale in relief that he seems to have eased off tracking my every move, and that I'll have time to prepare alone for the event tonight. I'll be on display to all of Sebastian's colleagues and family, and I'm determined to make an impact.

And bring every conflict between them to a boil.

* * *

Back at the house, I get ready for the party, styling my hair, doing my makeup, and picking an outfit from the half-dozen gorgeous dresses I picked up at London's best boutiques. I deliberate between demure pink silk, and dramatic burgundy red, before selecting the red. I'm tired of playing the innocent all day, and my instincts tell me, Sebastian will want to turn heads tonight.

And this dress? It's a head-turner, for sure: a long, strapless satin gown, slit to mid-thigh, with a classic Hollywood vibe. Pairing it with sky-high matching heels and diamond earrings, I leave my hair down in waves. I remove my bandages from my wrists; the scars are still visible, but I cover them with two chunky cuffs in hammered gold, so they're hidden out of sight.

There. I check out my reflection in the mirror, pleased at the glamorous effect. I tell myself that this is all part of my act, blending in with the social elites, but I can't deny that there's a small part of me hoping that Sebastian will like the outfit, too.

And not just to keep his obsession with me alive.

The driver arrives right at seven, and I head to the party alone. It's taking place at a luxurious hotel, and I'm ushered out into the huge, private courtyard, which is already packed with guests.

"Champagne?" a staff member materializes with a tray.

I take one and sip, absorbing the scene. The courtyard is nestled amongst the tall skyscrapers and office buildings, like a small piece of history with its manicured hedges and crumbling stonework. It's been decorated with a private dancefloor and lavish floral arrangements, and there's a full bar and jazz band playing, and staff circulating with delicious-looking canapés, as the chic, stylish crowd mingles and chats.

I take a deep breath. Despite looking the part, I'm way out of my comfort zone among these people, and it's harder to fake my way through it without Sebastian at my side. So, I head for the buffet spread instead, and kill time filling a plate with food, even though I know I'm too tense to eat.

"Avery!"

I hear my name and turn in time to see a familiar face across the courtyard. It's Lulu, the journalist I met last month, and my first official friend in London.

At least, as much a friend as I can have, when I'm scheming about Sebastian's every move.

"Hi!" I wave back, and she weaves her way through the crowd towards me. It's not easy, considering how packed the space is, but she arrives with a sigh.

"Oh my God, talk about a scrum. I nearly elbowed the Duchess of Sussex in the neck!" Lulu gives me a hug, and air kisses, beaming. She's wearing a cute black cocktail dress, with a sparkly fascinator headband. "You look stunning!"

"Thanks," I smile, striking a little pose. "I figured, why not? Drink?" I ask, grabbing her a glass.

"Just the one," Lulu demurs. "Technically, I'm working. Covering the party for the society pages," she explains. "My editor warned me to keep my mouth shut, and blend into the scenery."

"How's that going?" I ask, smiling at her infectious energy.

"Too well!" she exclaims. "I've had three people ask me to fetch more canapés."

I laugh. "Think of it as being deep undercover," I advise. "You never know what people will say in front of the staff."

"Ooh, good point. So... Is Sebastian here?" Lulu asks, eagerly looking around.

I hide a smirk. As much as I enjoy Lulu's company, I can't forget that she has an agenda, too. She's longing to get promoted off the society pages and be a more serious journalist... Which means she's got her eyes open for a scoop, too.

"He's meeting me here. Got tied up at work."

"That's right," Lulu's eyes widen. "The Dunleavey takeover. How is that working out?"

She tries to sound casual, but I can tell, she's angling for information.

I give a careless shrug, eating a canapé. "Oh, who knows? I glaze over when Seb starts talking business, you know, it's all merger this, and layoffs that. So dull."

"Right." Lulu manages a laugh. "The worst!"

I want to laugh, both of us pretending we couldn't care less about the high stakes of Wolfe Capital and the finance world, when really, we both are dying to uncover a scandal.

Which is why I'm keeping Lulu close. Our interests align, and one of these days, we'll be very useful to each other.

"So, tell me, where have you been?" Lulu asks, as we stroll around the party. "I left you a bunch of messages!"

I wince. "I know, I'm so sorry!" I can't exactly tell her that my phone was taken away while I was locked up in Larkspur, so I tell an easy lie. "I was at this amazing retreat for the past couple of weeks," I lie, "They do the whole 'reconnecting with your inner self' thing, and part of that is no cell phones."

"That sounds awesome." Lulu sighs. "You're so lucky."

I think of the hell of Larkspur and give a wry laugh. *Sure, lucky.* "Anyway, I actually missed the real world," I say. "It's good to be back!"

"Well, it's good to have you." Lulu grins. "Let's get lunch soon."

"Absolutely," I agree.

She finishes her champagne. "Well, I guess I better walk around and get all the hot gossip. How would our readers cope if they didn't hear about Rachel Featherington-Stone's new line of vegan leather handbags? Or Imogen Hawthorne's charity luncheon to raise funds for impoverished Chihuahua dogs?"

I laugh. "Still looking for your big scoop to get promoted?" I ask.

"Yup. So if you catch someone doing something naughty behind the rosebushes..."

I chuckle. "I promise, you'll be the first to know."

Lulu disappears into the crowd, but our short conversation has helped me relax, and I grab another champagne flute from the tray of a passing waiter before making my way further into the courtyard.

There's a jazz band set up on the cobblestones off to the side, and the music adds an extra layer of excitement to the party. Not that it needs it. I was right; everyone is dressed up in designer dresses and tailored suits with expensive jewelry, greeting each other with thrilled exclamations. Their conversation drifts over to me: talk of yacht trips, and boarding schools, and skiing in the Alps...

It's another world here, for sure.

A hand sliding across my bare back makes me jump. I whirl around to find Sebastian's uncle, Richard, giving me a smarmy grin. "Avery, you look stunning," he says, and it's not just a general compliment. The words are accompanied by a lingering gaze on my chest that makes my skin crawl.

"Thank you," I say lightly, stepping back, out of his reach. "And congratulations. On the anniversary."

To your dead brother's wife.

Richard glances around. "And where's my nephew?"

"He supposed to meet me here, but I don't think he's arrived yet."

"Of course." Richard smarms. "That boy always did have a tendency to be careless about other people's time."

"I'm sure he's busy with something important," I reply, not to defend Sebastian, but to see if I can get under Richard's skin. There's definitely friction between them, and I want to play it up. "He does such a good job at the company," I add, sunny. "It's no wonder everyone there worships him."

Richard's smile turns brittle. "What an interesting way of putting it. Then again, it's a thin line between respect and fear."

"Really?" I ask, sounding innocent. "And which one do you feel towards Seb?"

Richard blinks, surprised at the question. Then the smarmy smirk returns. "Well, I certainly have nothing to fear from that man..."

Interesting. From what I've seen, there's not a man in London who doesn't quake in his boots at the thought of Sebastian's wrath, so what makes Richard so confident?

I feel an awareness rush over my skin, and I know I'm being watched. Turning, I see Sebastian making his way through to crowd toward us, his eyes flickering between me and Richard.

"There you are," I greet him brightly. "We were just talking about you."

When Sebastian reaches us, he slips an arm around my waist and pulls me as close as possible. It feels like he's staking a claim on me. "Is that so?" he asks, giving Richard a cool, assessing look.

"All good things," I add, amused. "Did you get everything settled at work?"

He gives a brisk nod.

"It's nice of you to join us," Richard says, "I would hate to see you disappoint your mother. Again."

Ouch.

"Well, you know how it is," Sebastian replies casually. "I'm running a business. There's always a mess to clean up these days, what with all the interference going on. People sticking their noses where they don't belong."

Double ouch.

Richard's smile gets stiff. "I would think you'd appreciate the help. Wolfe Capital is a big responsibility. A legacy to live up to."

"Yes. My *father's* legacy." Sebastian says, brittle.

"Among others," Richard is quick to reply.

I glance back and forth, tracking every barbed comment and sign of tension. I feel like I should have popcorn right now, for the show these men are putting on for me.

"That's right," Sebastian says, scornful. "There is your brief tenure to think about. Funny how many poor decisions can be made in such a short period of time. Did you know, darling, that my uncle ran the company for a while?"

I look innocent. "Really?"

"Of course, 'ran' is being generous," Sebastian continues. "The only thing he did was almost drive it into the ground before I took over."

"I was a steady hand," Richard replies, sounding angry.

"You played it safe," Sebastian shoots back, almost mocking. "But that was always the difference between you and my father, wasn't it? He was willing to take risks, and make his own name, instead of riding on the coattails of somebody else's?"

"And how did that work out for him? I don't see him here tonight, do you?"

Woah.

I blink at the insult. "I'm starving!" I blurt, quickly interrupting. I place a hand on Sebastian's arm, feeling the tension coiled in his muscles. "Let's go get something to eat."

Sebastian doesn't move.

"Baby?" I coo, tugging gently. "Let's not make a scene," I murmur softly. Sure enough, people are glancing over, clearly reading the body language, even if nobody can hear their conversation.

Sebastian gives an abrupt nod. "Fine."

I flash a fake smile at Richard, and steer Sebastian away. "Well, he's a fucking asshole," I curse cheerfully, leading Sebastian to a quiet spot, away from the crowd.

He looks at me, then barks a surprised laugh. "I can't believe you just said that."

"Well, he is." I shrug. "I know he's family, and all, but still…"

Sebastian seems to relax a little at that. His gaze sweeps over me and turns appreciative. "I like this dress," he says, tracing the low neckline.

"Good." I smile back at him. "You paid for it."

"Worth every penny," he says immediately. "Buy ten more."

I laugh. "You know what else you bought today?" I say, dropping my voice. "The lingerie I'm wearing underneath."

I'm expecting that to put all thoughts of his family firmly

out of mind, but instead, Sebastian gives me a thoughtful look. "Are you trying to distract me?"

Busted.

"What could you possibly need distracting from?" I ask lightly. "This lovely, not-at-all weird party, full of your close friends, and beloved family, that you clearly adore?"

He snorts with laughter. "How long do you think we need to stay?" he asks, draping an arm around my shoulder and pulling me close.

I feel a strange glow, nestled in his embrace as we look out at the party. It almost feels like we're partners. In this together.

"Long enough for me to eat my body weight in these crab puffs," I reply. "Have you tried them?"

I bring one to his mouth, and he takes a bite.

"They're good," he nods. "How about I just write the caterer a check and have a hundred delivered to the house?"

I laugh. "Have you ever met a problem you couldn't buy your way out of?"

He looks right at me.

"You."

My heart stops, and the air between us suddenly crackles with intensity. He holds my gaze, and there's something there in the icy blue depths I don't think I've ever seen before. A glimpse of respect, and affection.

Then there's the sound of a clinking glass, and he looks away. The moment is lost.

"Thank you all for joining us, to celebrate tonight..."

It's Richard, up by the bandstand with Sebastian's mother, Trudy, on his arm. They're beaming together, clearly about to make some kind of speech.

I glance back at Sebastian, who's watching with a stony expression, all his good humor gone again.

"It's hard to believe that I'm here, celebrating my twelve

years of happiness with this beautiful woman," Richard says, gesturing to Trudy, who looks at him with stars in her eyes. "I can't help thinking about how lucky I am. Of all things, tragedy brought us together. It might seem strange but finding comfort in each other gave us a new beginning that we desperately needed."

I can't believe they're really doing this: Framing Sebastian's father's death as the reason they got together. I can't imagine how Sebastian must be feeling, and even though it looks like he's just sipping his champagne, nodding along to the speech, there's a storm brewing in his eyes, emotion roiling beneath the surface that he's obviously trying to hide.

A man like Sebastian Wolfe will *always* hide that side of himself. I know him well enough to know that.

I squeeze his hand. "Let's get out of here," I whisper.

He blinks at me, surprised.

"I mean, we have the catering number," I add. "What else do we need?"

He sucks in a breath, and glances to the stage again, where Richard is still going strong, talking about partnership, and love, and destiny.

"Fine," he says, almost a growl. "Let's go."

We melt into the crowd and make a discreet exit, emerging from the hotel entrance. I look around. It's still early, and I'm all dressed up. "How about we go get dinner?" I suggest, as the car pulls up.

"No..." Sebastian gives me an unreadable look. "I have something else in mind."

OK then.

We get in the car, and Sebastian leans forward to murmur an address to the driver. Then he pulls out his phone and taps out a message, before tucking it away.

"So what's the plan?" I ask.

Sebastian doesn't answer me. Instead, he opens a compartment in the car, and pulls out a slim black jewelry box. "I have something for you," he says, handing it to me.

I take it, pausing. There's a look in his eyes I can't decipher, and the energy around him has changed now that we're away from the party. It's sharper; alert. Poised for something.

My pulse rises as I open the box. Nestled inside is a stunning diamond choker.

"It's gorgeous!" I exclaim, lifting it out. Then I see, there's a silver ring hanging from the front, and...

A long, supple leather band beneath it in the box.

Is that...

A leash?

I gasp, shooting Sebastian a tremulous look. He's watching me, still unreadable.

"Let me see it on you," he says, in a quiet command.

I do as he says, fastening the choker around my neck with trembling hands.

Sebastian lifts the leather leash from the box, and carefully fastens it to the necklace. He wraps the leather around one fist, holding the leash lightly in his hand.

My leash.

Holy shit.

My body floods with heat, and I'm suddenly breathless with anticipation.

Sebastian slowly adjusts the diamonds, and gives me a cool, cryptic smile. "There. Now you're ready."

But ready for what?

I have no idea what's going to happen next, but oh, I'm already wet and aching between my thighs, shocked by his casual domination—and how much it thrills me.

This is going to be a night I'll never forget.

Chapter 7

Sebastian

I've been on edge all day, and that twisted excuse for a celebration party hasn't helped. Watching my uncle and my mother fawn all over each other, and the way that Richard brought up the accident as if it's all just part of their love story together...

Let's just say it wasn't ideal.

"Where are we going? Am I supposed to wear this?" Avery's breathless questions pull me back to the present and give me focus, as the car glides to a stop.

We're here. Good.

I take a breath, enjoying the flush on her cheeks, and how she's toying with the diamond collar, looking nervous and turned on all at once. She might not be as innocent as I once thought, but it's clear, she's never worn anything like this before.

I smile, already anticipating the night to come.

The things I'm going to show her. All the ways I'll make her beg.

Her pleasure is exquisite, and we haven't even scratched the surface of her desire.

I rest a hand on her leg, calming her. "Relax," I tell her. "You'll see."

The driver opens my door, and I get out, leading Avery after me. I've taken her by the hand, not the leash on her pretty collar, I don't want to overwhelm her right away. But still, that dark sense of possession is already twisting to life inside me, and just the sight of her so wide-eyed and eager to learn is making me hard.

But I have big plans for tonight.

We're at the back entrance to a nondescript townhouse in an exclusive part of the city. There are no signs or markings at the door, but when I push it open, a beautiful woman dressed in a designer gown greets me immediately. "Welcome," she says expectantly.

I produce a slim card with my membership. She smiles. "Please, go right ahead. Let me know if there's any way I can be of service to you, tonight..."

Her gaze lingers, but I'm not interested in her services. Avery is the only one I'm focused on, as I take her by the hand and lead her down the elegant hallway, to where the space opens into a dimly lit bar area. It's styled like an old-fashioned speakeasy, all Art Deco gilt edgings and brocade wallpaper, with a polished bar and liquor bottles glinting from a mirrored wall. Tonight, there are a couple of dozen people already here, in pairs and groups, murmuring hushed conversation in dim corners.

Avery follows me, looking eagerly around. "Oh, this place is cute," she says, sounding relieved, and I smile at her innocence.

Then her eyes adjust to the dim lights, and her pretty lips drop open in surprise.

"I..." she clutches my hand tighter. "They're... Um..."

"Fucking?" I reply. There's a couple nearby, half-hidden in the shadows in one of the booths, already enjoying their evening. The man is sitting back, arms on the back of the booth, sipping a drink as his companion rides him, her dress rucked up around her waist, and her bare breasts bouncing with every slow thrust.

Avery watches them in clear disbelief. "What is this place?" she whispers, drawing closer to me.

"What do you think it is?" I reply.

"A... sex club?" she blurts, blushing prettily.

"One of the most exclusive sex clubs in the world," I confirm.

"Oh." Avery swallows. "But it's so classy," she whispers, eyes darting around. "I would never have guessed, if it wasn't for, you know..."

The man on his knees by the bar, patiently waiting for his mistress to finish her conversation. The woman in a dark corner, sandwiched between two men. The couple slow dancing under the crystal chandelier, as he massages her breasts through her elegant gown.

"That's the point," I tell her, as I steer her across the room. "And what we pay an exorbitant membership fee to enjoy."

"So, you've come here before?" Avery's gaze darts back to me.

I nod. "From time to time."

"So, that hostess in reception..." her face changes, and I feel a strange burn of satisfaction.

"Jealous, Sparrow?" I tease.

She flushes deeper. "No. I just... You know I've never been anywhere like this before. How am I supposed to act?"

"However you like." I say, sitting at a table that faces the room. I gesture a waiter over, and order drinks, as Avery perches on a chair beside me, sneaking looks around the room.

"You don't need to be ashamed," I tell her, amused by her caution. "Everyone is here because they want to be. To be seen, to watch, to enjoy... You remember how that felt, don't you?" I add, remembering our night at the party in Notting Hill, and how I touched her on the balcony where anyone could see.

She was so wet for me, hating the public display—but going wild for it, all the same.

And Avery remembers too. Her pupils dilate, and she wets her lips, her breath coming faster. "Is that what you want to do with me here?" she asks.

I pause, enjoying her suspense.

"That depends," I reply finally, tracing a fingertip over her bare arm. She shivers like a live wire beneath my touch. "Is that what you'd like, darling?" I murmur, leaning closer. "For me to touch you right here, in the middle of this bar where everyone can see? Or perhaps you'd like to serve me tonight. Get down on your knees in that pretty diamond collar and suck my cock so everyone knows what a good little girl you can be."

Avery's body shudders, and I can practically see her clench that sweet cunt beneath her gown.

"I..." she stammers, eyes going glazed. "I..."

I sit back, smirking. God, I love it when she's turned on like this. A servant to her body's secret yearnings, she doesn't even realize how her desire is written all over her face—and body, and stiff nipples, poking at the satin of her gown.

"Think about it, why don't you?" I suggest casually. "Enjoy our company tonight. Perhaps you'll be... Inspired."

Our drinks arrive, and Avery gulps hers down as if she's parched. I can already see her busy mind working overtime, trying to assess what to do and how to play this.

She doesn't realize yet, I'm the one in control.

Tonight—and always. She made her choice, and she chose to stay with me. And now... Now I'll give her the surrender she craves. Demand her submission, and revel in every moment of it.

But after everything that's happened these past few weeks, I need to be sure. I have to know if I can trust her.

And tonight, I'm going to find out.

Avery's head turns. Across the bar, a beautiful blonde woman is moving towards the booth, where the first couple is still intertwined. The blonde slides in beside them, reaching up to kiss the brunette girl even as she still straddles her partner.

The three of them embrace, heads dipping towards each other, tongues lingering as they trade kisses. The blonde peels the other woman's dress lower, and bends her head, sucking and licking her breasts until the brunette is moaning, grinding on the man's lap, taking her pleasure from his cock.

Avery exhales a shaking breath. She can't look away. I can see the arousal in her expression, her lips parted, a blush on her cheeks. Her eyes are wide, and I know that if I slipped a hand up her dress, I'd find her wet and ready for me.

"Come here," I murmur, patting my lap.

Avery jolts, but she immediately obeys, getting up and circling the table to perch on my lap, facing the room.

I pull her closer, so she's sitting with her back flush against my chest, and my arms encircling her.

"Do you like what you see?" I whisper, trailing my hands over her bare arms.

She doesn't reply, but her whole body is trembling. Overwhelmed.

"I think you do..." I muse. "I think it turns you on, *watching*. Because we already know, you liked to be watched, don't you, Sparrow?"

Slowly, deliberately, I place a hand on each of her knees, and ease them open.

She gasps, her body going tense. Her skirt still covers her, but she tries to close her legs.

I grip them firmly, holding her open.

"Shh..." I whisper, trailing kisses down the pale column of her throat. "Don't you want everyone here to see this beautiful body?"

Avery looks out at the room, and tenses. "Sebastian... They're looking."

"So they are," I say, pleased. People are watching us now, sending curious glances over to our table. I can see their eyes widen in recognition at me, in shock and awe. I'm usually more discreet than this, keeping my activities to the private rooms and dark corners of the club, but tonight, I won't be hiding anything.

I'm staking my claim to Avery, where everyone can see.

I move one hand to her chest, teasing and toying with one breast through the fabric of her dress.

"But...We can't..." Avery wriggles in my lap, the movement going straight to my cock.

"We can't what?" I ask, amused that she's still fighting this. But that's how all our lessons have unfolded. First, the denial, where she clings to innocence. Then, the surrender to her true desire.

And how fucking sweet that surrender is.

I pluck her nipple, hard, and Avery sounds a muffled whimper of pleasure, arching a little into my palm.

"Do... *This*," she breathes faster, even as she grinds again on my thick cock.

"You can... And you will."

I keep her pinned in place on my lap as I ease her dress down, revealing her bare breasts, pale in the dim light. "So pretty..." I murmur approvingly, tracing her nipples until they jut out in two stiff peaks. "I think our audience likes them, too."

Avery tenses at the reminder, and she strains to see the people watching us, openly enjoying the show. We're not hidden in the shadows like last time, where only an accident would make someone glance her way.

She's on display to them now. My trophy. Splayed on my lap with her legs open and her juicy breasts bared, whimpering for my touch even as she shudders in shame.

I kiss her neck, and slowly massage her breasts, teasing them in the way I know drives her crazy. "Can you moan for them, baby? Show them all how good it feels."

Avery pants for breath. I can feel the war playing out inside her, between decency and pleasure.

Pleasure wins.

She moans out loud, a filthy, desperate sound that echoes through the hushed room.

Triumph burns in my chest.

"Good girl," I rasp, opening her legs wider. "Now, let's see how wet this pussy gets, putting on a show."

I peel her skirt back until her legs are draped wide over my lap, revealing a scrap of damp silk stretched taut over her core.

I touch her softly, and she shudders against my hand.

"You're soaked," I groan in satisfaction. "My good girl loves everyone watching her come undone."

Avery moans again, her head back against my shoulder, her body arching into my hands. "Please..." she whispers.

"You want more?" I tease her, only brushing my knuckles against her soaking panties. "You want me to touch you here, while everyone watches?"

"Yes," she gasps, writhing. "Oh God, I shouldn't but... *Yes.*"

I tug her panties down, and off her body, baring her to the world. Fuck, she's so wet, glistening in the dim light as I swipe through her juices.

All eyes are on us as I begin to rub her clit in slow strokes, drawing more desperate moans from her mouth.

Fuck, this girl is intoxicating.

I've known envy, what it's like to have people covet what you possess. My house, my cars, my business... But I swear, nothing is as potent as the jealousy being sent in my direction tonight. Every man in this room, and half the women too, are burning up with envy, watching Avery draped and whimpering in my lap with her legs spread and her wet pussy clenching for the whole room to see.

I feel like a fucking god.

I sink a finger into her tight cunt, and fuck, the way she grips up around it makes me want to throw her down and fuck her right now.

Patience.

I add another finger, flexing them, and already she's sobbing, gasping, trying to ride my hand toward her climax.

"Are you going to come for me, darling?" I ask, my voice rough with self-control because fuck, what I wouldn't give to be buried balls-deep in this tight pussy right now. "Are you going to show these people who owns your cunt?"

She sounds a strangled moan, half out of her mind with pleasure.

I thrust my fingers deeper, eyes drifting over the attentive crowd. I had a suspicion she'd love the voyeuristic thrill of a public display like this, but I never dreamed she'd take me so eagerly, body heaving, the dirty shock of it all driving her to what I already know will be a mammoth climax.

I catch sight of a familiar face in the crowd, and smile.

Right on time.

"Tell them," I command her. "Tell them who you belong to."

"Sebastian..." she gasps. I angle my hand to grind against her clit. She sobs louder, shuddering in my arms. "Sebastian!"

"That's right. You're mine," I growl, squeezing her breast tightly. "Your body exists for my pleasure. Your climax is a gift you have to earn. And believe me, the night is only just getting started. So show them, show them who makes you scream. *Come.*"

As I issue the ragged command, I withdraw my fingers, and slap her clit. Hard.

Avery shatters with a shocked scream, her whole body writhing and jerking in my arms with the force of her orgasm. I hold her there, displaying her pleasure to the room as her cries echo and her limbs flail.

Bringing her to climax is always a victory, but this one is especially sweet. And not just because of the audience here, to bear witness to her surrender.

She has no idea what's still to come.

Finally, Avery stills, gasping. I lift her to her feet, adjusting her dress. She's gazing at me in a daze, her face a picture of pleasure.

But I'm not done yet.

"Follow me," I order her softly. Then I take the leather leash connecting to her collar and lead her from the room. Our audience is forgotten, they've served their purpose now.

Avery follows, stumbling a little on unsteady feet as I take her down the hallway, and back to one of the private rooms I've reserved for the evening.

I close the door behind us.

"Take it off," I demand, pointing to her dress. I'm impatient now, the fire in my blood at boiling point, a savage heat that won't be contained for long.

Avery tries to catch her breath. She fumbles with the dress, shaking, and I can see she's still reeling from what just happened out in the bar.

She doesn't realize, it's only a taste of what's in store for her tonight.

The red satin drops to a pool on the floor, and I groan in appreciation.

She blushes, and I remember how much she thrives on my praise. "You like it?" she asks, striking a bashful little pose.

Naked, she's a fucking work of art. Long, lush legs, a rounded ass, and those magnificent tits...

"Get on the bed," I order her roughly, leading her to it by the leash.

She follows my orders eagerly, kneeling on the sheets, her eyes wide with anticipation. Her gaze moves to my groin, where my hard-on is jutting through my pants. She wets her lips. "Will you let me please you?" she asks in a soft whisper, and fuck, it's like a choir of angels.

"Oh, you'll please me, alright," I vow.

Then the door opens.

Avery turns, eyes widening in surprise and confusion as my friend, Saint, strolls into the room.

"Starting without me?" he drawls, amused. "That's not very polite."

"Don't worry," I say casually. "You're right on time."

Avery scrambles to try and cover herself, her head turning back and forth between us. I can see the questions on her innocent face, and I'll admit, it makes me even harder.

"No," I stop her. "Don't hide. Show him your beautiful body."

Saint moves closer. "Gorgeous," he says, approving. "We're going to have some fun tonight."

Avery meets my eyes, shocked. "What does he mean?" she asks in a whisper. "Sebastian? What's going on?"

"It's time for your next lesson, Sparrow," I say, handing Saint the leash. I stroll to the chair beside the bed, and settle back, ready for the show.

To see just how far Avery is willing to submit to me.

"My friend here is going to fuck you. And I'm going to watch."

Chapter 8

Avery

I feel like I'm dreaming.

One of those sexy, forbidden dreams, beyond anything you could imagine in waking life. The kind of dream that leaves you gasping in pleasure, waking in a hot sweat with the sheets soaked and your body aching for release.

But this isn't a dream.

And I'm already wide awake.

"You want me... and him... to...?"

I stare at Sebastian in shock, reeling from the filthy promise of his words. I'm still shaken from the force of my climax, and what Sebastian just did to me —with me—out there in the club for everyone to see.

But now we're behind closed doors. The three of us.

Me, Sebastian, and...

Saint.

His friend. Darkly handsome, wildly arrogant. An aristocrat, through and through. And now the man holding the leash attached to my diamond collar, a lazy smile on his face.

I gulp, looking back and forth between them. Sebastian is

lounging back in the armchair, clearly in control, while Saint's eyes are drifting over my naked body, full of anticipation. They're both so relaxed about this, as if it's just a regular Friday night to share a woman.

They've done this before.

I inhale in a rush. "Are you sure?" I ask Sebastian. Aside from the shock of his dirty command, I'm surprised.

Sebastian Wolfe isn't a man who likes to share. From the moment we met, he's made it clear that I belong to him. And anyone who dares touch his possessions will pay the price for it.

But now, Sebastian relaxes, his eyes burning into me. "Oh yes," he says calmly. "You said you wanted to please me. Well, this will be for both our pleasures, Sparrow."

I shiver.

There's something going on here, more than just a wild sexual adventure. And as Sebastian leans forward onto his elbows, his gaze fixed on me, I see something beneath the surface. A question.

A challenge.

Suddenly, I realize... *This is a test.*

Despite everything we've been through—or maybe because of it. Sebastian is testing me. Seeing just how far I'll go at his command.

What I'll do to please him.

I can't fail.

I swallow hard and give a tiny nod. "If it's what you want," I tell him.

Beside me, Saint chuckles. "You needn't be a martyr," he teases me gently, a look of mischief in his eyes. "I won't bite."

He leans down, breath hot on my cheek. "At least, not until you're begging for it."

He kisses me suddenly, and I startle at the unfamiliar touch. Sebastian's kisses are demanding, full of intensity, but

Saint's mouth is slow and thorough, almost leisurely as his tongue explores me. His lips are different, fuller, and I can feel his playful smile against me as his hands slide over my body, laying me down on the bed.

"You're right," he says, finally pulling away and turning to where Sebastian is watching us. "She's delicious."

"So taste her," he orders.

"Bossy bastard, isn't he?" Saint says, grinning at me, his hands still stroking shivers from my skin. "I don't know how you put up with it, all 'Yes sir,' 'No sir'."

"Hey," Sebastian growls.

"Hush you," Saint smirks over to him. "I'm busy."

He dips his head to lick across my breasts, closing his mouth around one nipple to suck.

Oh God.

Is this really happening? I can't believe it—but my body can, already arching towards Saint's teasing touch.

I turn my head, looking to Sebastian for reassurance. Permission.

He gives a dark nod, getting to his feet. One hand already moving to unsnap his belt, and free his hard, thick cock to stroke, watching his friend's mouth rove across my naked skin.

He wants this, too.

And just like that, I relax, surrendering to the wild, unbelievable experience, and the unfamiliar pleasure of Saint's mouth on my breasts.

It's incredible, the filthy, forbidden rush of this situation. I'd be lying if I said I'd never fantasized about this: two men, their attention on me. Their hands... their bodies...

My anticipation builds, as Sebastian approaches us. He trails a hand over my face, sinking his thumb into my mouth for me to suck.

I do it, eagerly, as Saint toys with my nipples, making me moan.

"So sweet," Saint laps my nipple approvingly.

"Her pussy's even sweeter," Sebastian's voice comes, rough.

"Is it now?" Saint arches a wicked eyebrow at me. "We'll just have to see about that."

He moves down the bed, trailing his tongue over my sensitive skin, making me arch and gasp.

Sebastian turns my head. I'm level with his crotch, as he shoves down his pants. His cock springs free, hard and eager. "Suck it," he demands, still gripping my jaw. He presses his thumb down, forcing my mouth wider. "Show Saint how you swallow my cock, while he gorges on your pussy."

I moan, shaking. Fumbling to reach for him and lick his thick shaft. Sebastian doesn't wait, he thrusts into my mouth roughly, as Saint suddenly buries his face between my legs.

I cry out around Sebastian's cock as Saint licks hard against my clit.

Holy shit!

The sensations are overwhelming: Saint's mouth, cool and foreign at my core, his tongue lazily toying with my stiff bud as Sebastian crams his thick cock down my throat. I choke, gagging at the invasion, but he doesn't ease up, he just thrusts again, gripping my leash to pin me there in place as Saint sends pleasure soaring through my body with every flick and suck.

It's too much, too good, all at once.

It's *everything*.

I swear, my brain shuts off, I can't process it all. I give myself up completely to the animal thrusts of Sebastian's cock, burying himself in my throat, as his friend makes me whimper and moan, lapping at my clit. My body is electric, overstimulated, flying towards the edge—

"Don't let her come," Sebastian orders, yanking me up off

his cock. I gasp for air, panting and drooling, as Saint lifts his head from my pussy.

"Oh, but she's so close..." he smirks, lazily flicking his tongue against my clit.

I cry out, arching towards him, trembling with tension.

"See?" Saint smiles. "I bet she looks so pretty when she comes."

"She's even prettier when she begs for it," Sebastian growls. "Don't you want to try her mouth?"

"Good point."

Saint nips my thigh, and then rises, stripping off his pants and shirt. He kneels above me, his cock jutting from his naked body.

My eyes drink him in. He's toned, an athlete's body, with a tangle of dark chest hair and a well-defined V leading down to...

"She likes it," Saint smirks, casually fisting his cock. "Maybe she's been missing out."

"Don't even start." Sebastian growls.

"Oh, relax. C'mon, baby," he says, guiding it to my open mouth. "Time to get me nice and wet for you."

I shudder at his words, as my lips close around his unfamiliar cock. He's thicker than Sebastian, the kind of girth that makes me choke, but Saint lets me get adjusted to the size of him, thrusting gently over and over, a little deeper each time, until he's buried balls-deep.

I hear his groan. "Fuck, that mouth... She feels like heaven."

"Yeah, she does." Sebastian leans down, holding my head in place, "Now open wide for him, Sparrow, and swallow every inch. Show him just how pretty you look with a cock in your mouth."

I moan, swallowing Saint down obediently, my head bobbing, still seized with heady pleasure from the whole experience. I dimly register hands on my body, moving me onto my hands and knees, where I can suck him more easily.

A sharp slap stings on my ass, and I gasp in surprise.

And pleasure...

"Easy there," Someone drags me off him, and then Sebastian's cock is waiting, still wet from my saliva. "Share and share alike."

He yanks me back to suck him again, and I moan, gripping my hands around both their cocks now, fisting them hard as I move my mouth between them, slobbering wetly, sucking each stiff dick down in turn.

"Good girl," I hear the fevered groans above me, and it sends fresh heat flooding my body.

"That's my good fucking girl."

Yes. *God yes.*

Hands roam my body, playing with my breasts, squeezing my nipples, making me moan and clench as I suck them down, losing track of whose cock I'm swallowing; whose palm is spanking my ass. It's a heady, frenzied chaos of groans and moaning, and my climax is building fast, my thighs trembling with need.

"Fuck, she's so wet." Saint groans. Fingers slide into me, dipping through my slick folds. "You're loving this, aren't you?"

I moan in agreement, as they pull me up, so I'm on my knees, sandwiched between them. Saint behind me, his mouth on the curve of my neck. His hands cupping my breasts, squeezing, pinching...

And Sebastian, right there in front of me. My face between his hands. His eyes burning into me, still the picture of control. "You've been such a good girl for me," he groans, claiming my mouth in a fierce, possessive kiss.

I melt into him, almost delirious, but glad for his familiar taste, and the solid weight of him, holding me up.

"Now, are you ready?"

"For what?" I manage, while words are still an option. Because the way Saint's hand is dipping between my legs, petting at me, slipping inside...

Oh God. I can't hold back, not like this.

Sebastian's hand glides to my throat, and softly squeezes.

"To be my good little whore."

I nearly come right then and there.

They lay me back, and Saint positions himself between my legs. "Is she going to be able to manage me?" he asks Sebastian, with a smirk.

"She can take it."

Sebastian's hands are on my wrists, pinning me down as Saint parts my thighs, I feel utterly overwhelmed—in the best way—reveling in the sense of surrender, being shared by them. Pleasured.

Used as they wish.

I brace myself for Saint's cock, but just as I feel his blunt head nudge at my entrance, Sebastian's grip on me tightens. "Stop!" he barks, yanking my body away.

Saint and I both look at him in surprise.

"You take her mouth," Sebastian growls, moving to replace Saint between my thighs. "I've changed my mind. This cunt belongs to me. And only me."

I barely have time to register the wild possession in his eyes before he slams inside, as if to prove his point. I cry out at the force of it. The exquisite friction, setting me alight.

"Oh my god!" I scream, shattering from the single thrust. "*Sebastian!*"

"That's right," he growls, thrusting into me again. Deeper. Thicker. Fucking me through my orgasm until I can't see straight for screaming. "I own you. Always. I'm the only one!"

As he pounds into me, rough hands turn my head, and Saint sinks his cock into my mouth again, every thick inch of it.

Oh God.

I suck him down, still coming, *coming*, choking on his cock as my body spasms in bliss from Sebastian's wild thrusts. Saint groans, hands in my hair, plunging deep. "Fuck, she's going off, I can feel it," he pants, "So fucking sexy, God, I'm going to come...."

Sebastian's fingers dig into my hips, he's panting, slowing his thrusts now. "Swallow it, Sparrow," he groans, wild-eyed. "Take all of his cum for me, be a good fucking girl."

I come again, with a whimper, pleasure slamming through me in fierce waves. God, will it end? I can't take it, the way these men are possessing every inch of me, their cocks demanding everything I have to give.

Saint's grip on my hair tightens, and then his cock is leaping in my throat, unleashing a torrent of hot liquid that makes me choke and gag. Still, I obey Sebastian and swallow every drop, as Saint curses and groans above me, whooping.

"Fuck, yes... *Fuck.*"

And then he's pulling free, pinning me down, holding me in place as Sebastian fucks me slowly, with an intensity that shakes me to my core. "Please," I gasp, eyes locked on Sebastian's. Begging for something I don't even know what. "*Please...*"

"What do you need, baby?" Saint croons in my ear. His hands are on my breasts, roving to pet my clit as Sebastian shifts, bringing my legs up over his shoulders and thrusting into me in a newly devastating angle.

So deep.

Too deep.

I sob with pleasure, as Saint strokes my clit, rubbing harder, and I cry out, arching off the bed towards them.

"This is your lesson, Sparrow, because this is what it feels like," Sebastian growls, his cock stretching me open with every new thrust. "To be *mine*. Mine to fuck. Mine to share. Mine to obey."

I give in to it willingly, delirious with pleasure. But Sebastian doesn't stop, not for a moment.

"You think you can't take it, but you will." He demands, face set in perfect control, even as his body takes on a new, animal frenzy. "Every inch. Every command. You'll surrender, because you know, it's what you *need*. You need to submit to me, just as much as I need to possess you. Completely."

Sebastian fucks into me again.

"Now *come*."

I couldn't deny him if I wanted to now, it's like my body knows he's won. I break apart one final time with an animal howl, pleasure slamming through me as Sebastian embeds himself to the hilt and grinds, grinds, *fuck*, coming into me with a roar as I shudder in his arms, my mind splintering from the force of his possession.

Because he's right.

This is what I've always needed, and never even known to want. My body and mind pushed past every limit. The freedom of total surrender.

My body is his.

But I swear, my heart never will be.

Chapter 9

Avery

The next morning, I sleep late, exhausted from my night of wild sexual debauchery. When I wake, it's only the pleasant ache of my body that tells me it wasn't just a dirty dream.

Was it really me who did those filthy things?

I look in the mirror and see that I'm blushing. It's no wonder, after everything I did with the two men last night. Moaning, begging, taking my pleasure from them—and offering up my body for them to enjoy in turn. I'm still flushed, my blood hot from the memories. I can't believe how much Sebastian is pushing me past my limits, or how good it feels. I never know what's going to come next with him, and that uncertainty is thrilling to me now, keeping me on this knife-edge, wondering what new lesson awaits.

When I go downstairs, Sebastian is just getting ready to leave for the office. He pauses in the foyer, smiling when he sees me coming down the stairs. "Good morning," he says.

I flush deeper, remembering the way he angled my body, drawing new cries of desire from my lips.

"Hi," I say, feeling strangely self-conscious. Of all the things we've done together, last night has left me feeling most exposed. Connected to him, somehow, in a deeper way.

"Did you sleep well?" he asks as I come to a stop in front of him. He reaches out to brush hair from my cheeks, his touch lingering softly.

Gentle.

I nod shyly. "I was pretty tired," I say, and he chuckles, pleased.

"You fell asleep in the car, I had to carry you up."

"Well, it was a big night," I blurt, my cheeks burning. I search his expression, wondering how he feels about me now, after everything we did.

Did I pass his twisted test?

"Yes, it was..." Sebastian's gaze is warm, and his touch affectionate as he pulls me closer for a gentle kiss. "No regrets, I hope?"

I blink in surprise at his affection. "No," I reply quickly, and it's the truth. I wouldn't take back one single moment of it.

"Good." Sebastian nods. "I'll be in the office today, but I'll be back for dinner."

"OK," I reply, and he drops another kiss to my lips. Not heated, or possessive, but something more casual. It's a goodbye kiss, like we're a real couple, and an unfamiliar kind of warmth spreads through me.

A sense of belonging...

I'm unsettled by the thought, but luckily, Leon the house manager enters. "Post came for you," he says, and then to my surprise, he offers me an envelope.

I pause, surprised. Who would be sending me mail here? Besides the threatening surveillance photos, I haven't received anything at the house.

I take the envelope, silently panicking. It doesn't look the same as the last delivery—this is just a small rectangle. Still, I can't be sure. "Thanks," I say brightly, hoping to open it in private.

But Sebastian looks curious, too. "Handing out 'change of address' cards?" he asks. My expression must be tense, because he adds an encouraging smile. "I'm only teasing. You're welcome to have anything sent here, now that you're staying. Go ahead."

He nods to the mail, and it sounds like an order.

Damn.

Refusing to open it now will just make him suspicious, so I tear the envelope, sending up a silent prayer—and then exhaling in relief when I see it's just an invitation, from what looks like a PR company.

'Courtesy of Charlie Ludlow PR,' the card reads.

Charlie... I realize that's the name Nero mentioned to me, his hacker contact who could help with my research. And the Barretti bar I ran for Nero back in New York?

It's on Ludlow Street.

"Well?" Sebastian asks, still waiting to know what my message is.

"Nothing important," I say, gladly showing off the card, which looks perfectly innocent. "I've just been invited to check out some fancy new spa experience."

Sebastian loses interest. "You can have my assistant handle invitations and promotional things," he says, collecting his briefcase. "I get dozens of those, every day. People begging me to try their new products," he rolls his eyes. "As if that's the way to prove their value."

"Thanks," I say, "But I'll take my free massage, thank you very much. I'm sure it'll be really relaxing."

And informative.

. . .

I get ready and head out to the address on the invitation, not exactly sure what to expect from this cloak-and-dagger secret meeting with Charlie. The last thing I would have guessed is that it would be the Met Police Headquarters. I'm standing in front of the building, trying to figure out what my next move should be, when a female voice startles me.

"You're late."

I whirl around, surprised. A young woman is standing there, in her mid-twenties, maybe. She's wearing a leather jacket and jeans with lace-up boots, dark eyeliner smudging her lashes, and her long auburn hair caught up under a black knit cap.

"Um, hi?" I ask, confused. I look around, but the street is just full of people going about their business.

"You're Avery." She says it like a statement, not a question, with a faint American accent.

"Yes..." I swallow, nervous. Did I get this wrong? Is it a trap? "I'm looking for Charlie?" I ask hesitantly, and the girl nods.

"You've found me."

"Oh." I blink, processing the news. *This* is Nero's expert hacker? "Sorry, I was just expecting..."

"A geeky dude who hasn't seen sunlight in the past twenty years," Charlie finishes for me, looking amused. "Yeah, I get that a lot. Come on," she turns on her chunky heels and starts walking—but not for the front entrance. She's heading to an alleyway that leads down the side of the building.

I hurry to catch up. "Where are we going?" I ask.

"I was told you need access to a police report."

She doesn't look at me as she speaks. Her eyes are casually scanning the area, and I have a feeling that she's taking in every single detail.

"Well, yes. I'm trying to find out more about a car accident, about fifteen years ago—"

"I don't need to know the whys," she interrupts me. We're walking along the side of the building now, trampling the grass. "I'm just here for the how."

Okay, then.

We come around the back of the building. There's a middle-aged officer near a back door, leaning against the wall with an unlit cigarette in his mouth.

When he sees Charlie coming, the man curses under his breath.

"No way," he grumbles, shaking his head as we approach. "I told you, it was one time."

Charlie grins. "That's what they all say," she says, teasing. "But they always come back begging for more."

She produces a silver lighter and lights the man's cigarette.

"You know I'm trying to quit," he tells her, sighing forlornly —and then taking a long drag. "Julie can't stand the smell."

"Mind over matter," she advises, friendly. "I know a great hypnotist, if you want."

He snorts. "Voluntarily go into a suggestive state, with one of your buddies? You're having a laugh. For all I know, you'll come out of the shadows, and program me to leave the front door unlocked." He looks over to me. "Word of advice, love, don't go leaving anything unattended around this one. She's liable to go looking where she doesn't belong."

"And there I was, thinking we were friends," Charlie protests, smiling widely. "Oh well, I guess I'll just have to find another friend to take these tickets for the big game on Saturday." She pulls something from her jacket and wafts them.

The police officer perks up. "What kind of tickets?"

"Good ones," she replies airily. "Corporate hospitality suite. Open bar. I'm sure Julie would have loved them..."

The cop gives her a look. "Out of the goodness of your heart, I'm sure."

"Of course." Charlie beams. "I just need a little favor..."

"Of course you do."

"Just a little peek at a report. Nothing classified. Come on," Charlie wheedles, still dangling the tickets. "No one has to know. It can be our secret."

"Your secrets will cost me my job," he grumbles, but he's already tossing his half-finished cigarette on the ground and stomping it out.

"That's why I appreciate it so much."

"Be quick about it, alright?" he mutters, leading us to the open door.

"Like the wind."

Charlie heads after him, and I follow, impressed by her skills of persuasion. The officer takes us down an industrial hallway, to a stairwell, and then down to the basement level.

I stay quiet, knowing that it's in my best interest not to draw any attention to myself whatsoever. I keep my head down and follow Charlie, glad that we don't encounter anyone along the way.

When we reach the bottom of the stairs, there's a room directly ahead with a sign on the door reading 'Records Department'. Inside, there are filing cabinets and shelves lining the walls of the small room, and a computer sits in the middle.

The officer takes a seat and clicks in his access codes. "File number?" he asks.

Charlie hands over a slip of paper, and the cop types it in, pulling up a file on the screen. "Vehicular accident..." He reads off the screen. "Look right to you?" he asks.

Charlie leans over. "That's the one."

He sends it to print, while he and Charlie chat about the soccer league, and his upcoming wedding anniversary. I keep an anxious eye on the door, certain we're about to get busted. Technically we're breaking into police HQ here, accessing private files... But Charlie doesn't seem nervous at all, like this is just a walk in the park as she scoops the file of the printer tray, and stuffs it in her jacket as we head upstairs again.

"Enjoy the game," she says breezily. "Send my love to Julie."

The cop just grumbles, closing the door behind us.

My mind is whirling as Charlie leads us a couple of blocks away. "I can't believe it was so easy to go strolling in there!" I exclaim, hurrying after her determined strides.

"You do know, we're trying to be discreet?" Charlie counters.

I shut up, until finally, we're on the empty back patio of a café nearby—the only two people braving the cold weather. Charlie brings us coffees, producing the file from her jacket.

"Voila," she says smugly.

I eagerly open the report, reading through each page as thoroughly as possible while Charlie sips her drink. I'm looking for something, anything, that might tell me more about the car accident that claimed Sebastian's father's life, or even hint at scandal, but as I scan the brief, printed summary, my hopes fade.

There's nothing.

Nothing except a stab of guilt, reading the awful details. What a tragic accident. Sebastian was only sixteen when it happened. I can't help wondering how he felt, learning the news that his father was gone...

I fight back my traitorous sympathy and put the report down with a sigh.

"No good?" Charlie asks.

I shake my head. "There's nothing new here. It's all the same vague information I've seen before: lost control of the vehicle, no foul play suspected, no trace of drugs or alcohol... I really thought there was more to the story than this."

"Let me see."

Charlie takes the pages, and starts reading, while I sit there feeling like I've hit yet another dead end.

Will I ever find a way to get my revenge?

I know someone as wealthy and powerful as Sebastian has the ability to cover up any scandals or weakness, but still, I was certain I could find *something* to use against him.

Nobody is untouchable. Not even him.

Charlie finishes her read with a wry look. "You're not wrong, it's hardly incriminating stuff. But you do have some new information."

I look up. "What are you talking about?"

She flips back to the first page of the report and places it in front of me again, pointing. "The name of the officer who was first on the scene. He's the one who wrote this riveting piece of police work, which means he would have seen the crash site for himself. It's not much, but it's something."

I read the name listed. "Terry Hardcastle."

Charlie pulls out her phone and starts scrolling. "Hmm, it looks like the guy took early retirement, a few years ago."

"So, we *are* out of luck?"

"No, it's the opposite." She explains. "If he's no longer with the force, he has no reason to lie to us. He's already got his pension; he's got nothing to lose. *If* there was anything more going on with this crash, then he's your best shot to get the unvarnished truth."

I like the way she thinks.

"What should I do next?" I ask, torn between hope—and more guilt, that I'm digging up these painful old ghosts.

"Nothing." Charlie sees my surprise. "From what I gather, you're not really in a position to go asking questions and digging up dirt, not with your busy social calendar," she adds lightly. "Sit tight and wait to hear from me. I'll find the guy and figure out your next move."

I nod. "OK. And... Thanks. I really appreciate the help."

Charlie gives me a look. "I owe Nero a couple of favors. Let's just say... He's helped me out of a scrape or two."

"He's good that way."

I get up to leave, but Charlie catches my arm. "Listen, I know I said I don't need to know the why, and I meant that. But... Sebastian Wolfe has a reputation," she says, giving me a careful look. "If he's got something buried, it's buried for a reason. And men like that... They'll do anything to protect their secrets."

I swallow hard.

"Thanks for the warning," I say, managing a smile. "But I know what I'm doing."

As I leave the café, I wonder if that's the truth. A couple of months ago, my mission seemed so clear. Now, it's growing more complicated by the day, clouded by questions—and my own traitorous desire for Sebastian.

But it's not just desire anymore...

As much as I hate to admit it, a deeper connection is forming between us, the more time I spend with him.

I had a chance to walk away, but for some reason I still don't understand, I didn't.

I *can't.*

The questions linger for the rest of my day. I walk for hours, dropping into a little bookstore, and spending time in some of my favorite London neighborhoods. I'm killing time, I know, until finally I head back to the house, my anticipation already growing.

Knowing I'll see Sebastian again.

When I get back, I hear his voice, coming from the office. I kick off my shoes, and pad down the hallway towards it.

His door is open, and I can see him sitting at his grand desk, reviewing paperwork with a look of total focus on his face.

Is it muscle memory that makes my stomach flip a little, watching him there? He's stripped off his jacket and loosened his tie, the sleeves of his white button-down shirt rolled up to reveal his tanned, strong forearms.

He glances up and sees me lingering in the doorway. "There you are," he says, pushing his hair back in a tired gesture. "Did you have a good day?"

"Mhmm," I give a vague murmur.

He beckons to me. "Come sit down a minute."

"Aren't you busy?"

"It can wait."

I slowly enter the office. He sits back, and gestures for me to sit on his lap, so I go to him, trying to ignore how familiar it already feels to nestle against his body, his arms encircling me.

"Long day crushing your enemies?" I ask, keeping my voice light, so the bitterness that's always hiding beneath my surface doesn't slip out.

But Sebastian gives a hollow laugh. "Not today. We've been doing a forensic audit of the whole damn company since Becca left."

I remember just in time to act surprised. "She's gone?" I ask. "I thought she was your trusty right hand."

"Yeah, well her hands were dipping into accounts that they didn't belong." Sebastian's voice is bitter. "After everything we'd been through, the opportunities I gave her..." He shakes his head. "I guess everyone has their price."

"I'm sorry," I say without thinking. But of course, after

working together so long, Sebastian would feel betrayed by her apparent crimes.

He sighs. "I don't know what accounts she's been stealing from, and if it's the Foundation..."

"What foundation?" I ask.

"I have a charity arm," he says absently. "Projects all over the world, focused on women's education and reproductive rights. It was one of my father's passions. It's an organizational mess, to be honest. Becca could have used the disarray to siphon funds, from the people who need them most."

Charity work? I feel a strange stab of guilt. It's the first I'm hearing about it. Which means I also know there'll be no money missing from those accounts – but I can't tell Sebastian that.

Besides, I want him distracted and overworked.

Don't I?

"I'll let you get back to work." I'm just about to get up and leave him when I glance at the spread of papers littering his desk.

A brown manila envelope is peeking out of a stack of papers, with what looks like my name scrawled in black marker on the front.

I freeze.

This one is like the first delivery: sized for photographs. *Do not bend.*

Oh god.

"What's this?" I ask, trying my best to sound calm as I pull it out of the stack. The envelope is still sealed shut, but that's no relief, when it was sitting right here for Sebastian to see.

"No idea, it was here when I got home," he replies.

Phew.

"Oh, I know!" I blurt, bouncing up. "It'll be the designs, for a dress I'm having made. I found this amazing designer, she's just out of fashion school, and I thought it would be fun to have something custom and one-of-a-kind."

My heart is pounding so loudly, I'm sure it'll give me away, but luckily, Sebastian's cellphone rings, distracting him.

He glances at the screen. "I need to take this."

"Of course," I blurt, backing towards the door. "Take your time!"

I hurry out of the room and up the stairs, clutching the envelope. It's not until the door is safely shut behind me, that I catch my breath, opening the seal.

It's more surveillance pictures.

Someone is still following me.

I suck in a breath, flipping through the black-and-white photographs. They're the same as last time—taken through a long-range lens, grainy but unmistakable. There I am on the sidewalk outside the library, talking to James. Leaving the house here. Strolling in the park.

I flip through them all, scared I'm going to find shots of me from today with Charlie at the Met HQ, but luckily, there's no sign of anything so incriminating.

Yet...

I reach the end of the photos and find another note. There are just three short words scrawled on the paper, but they make my blood run cold.

It's not over.

Chapter 10

Avery

I'm glad that Sebastian is so tired from working late, because I eat dinner alone, and then mouth a quick 'Goodnight' to him through the office door before disappearing off to bed.

Alone.

Not that I can sleep much. The photos are burning into my brain, even after I lit them on fire in my bathtub, burning them to ashes so they can never be found.

I thought I'd solved this problem.

I run over the possibilities all night, and by the time morning comes, I still have way too much pent-up nervous energy. So, I pull on my workout clothes and comfy tennis shoes, and head out for a jog. Maybe the physical activity and fresh air will help to clear my mind.

The morning air is foggy, which makes me feel more secure. It'll be hard to get good pictures of me with that going on, not that I'm doing anything worth photographing.

Are they tracking my every move?

I shiver, moving faster through the winding paths in the

nearby park. I've led such a sheltered life here in London that I'm running light on suspects, and I can't think of anyone who would want to threaten me like this.

At first, I was convinced my mystery stalker was Sebastian's old co-worker, Becca. Or at least that she was the one hiring someone to keep tabs on me. She even used the same phrases as the ones in my notes: Warning that she knew I wasn't as innocent as I seemed.

So I dealt with her, setting it up to look like she was embezzling from Wolfe Capital. As soon as Sebastian found out, he hit the roof, and fired her—plus threatened to unleash all kinds of legal trouble for her, too.

She was collateral damage, but I told myself it was worth it to save myself from being revealed. But now...

Now I realize, I got things very wrong. The photos aren't from Becca, she has no reason to still be coming after me.

Someone else must be doing it. Which means I have a whole new enemy out there.

What do they want from me?

I try to think logically. The fact I don't know many people here in town has to be a clue, in and of itself. The photographer must have staked me out for days before even catching me talking another man—

Wait a second.

I pause, catching my breath. I've been worried about the fact they photographed me at the library—proof that I'm not just shopping my days away like Sebastian believes. But somehow, they managed to catch me in conversation with James, too?

Literally the only time I've had a friendly conversation with a strange man, my entire time in London.

Make that *times*, plural. They photographed me with James again, the other day.

That can't be a coincidence.

I felt a jolt of excitement. This is my clue; it has to be.

I think back to when I first met James. He's the one that struck up a conversation with me initially, coming after me outside the library. He said I'd dropped a pen, and then suggested getting coffee. He asked me out that day, too, but I didn't think anything of it—he seemed so bashful and sweet.

And he's the one who reached over to pick some lint from my hair—at least, that's what he said he was doing. It just so happened to look from a distance like we were more intimate, comfortable with him touching me.

At the exact moment the photographer took their shots.

No, it *can't* a coincidence. How did I not see it before now?

James was a setup, from the start.

So what do I do now?

Impulsively, I pull out my phone. The slip of paper with his number is still tucked in a notebook in my pocket, so I dial it, my heart racing.

"Yeah?" The voice that answers sounds different, gruffer.

"James? This is Avery."

"Oh, hello. I'm glad you called, I was just thinking about you. Well, the mountains of research I have to do at the library, but that made me think of you."

There it is. The earnest, bashful voice I was expecting to hear. I'm surer than ever that it's an act.

He's not the only one who can pull off a performance.

"Oh dear," I say lightly. "That's not a great association. I'd much rather you're reminded by... I don't know, a nice sunny day, or a great cup of coffee."

He chuckles. "Well, according to my brainy friend, who's studying neuroscience, the only way to form new associations is write over our usual habits with new routines. Perhaps with lunch?"

Bingo.

"That sounds great," I say, pleased. "Text me the details."

"I can't wait."

We hang up, and a message comes through a minute later. He wants me to meet him at a restaurant near the library in a few hours. That gives me plenty of time to get ready. I pick up my jog again and head back to the house. When I get there, I'm surprised to see Sebastian coming down the stairs.

"What are you doing here?" I blurt out.

He arches an eyebrow.

"I just mean, I thought you were already at work. I was surprised, that's all. A good surprise," I add, covering. Luckily, I'm already flushed and breathless from my run, so hopefully, he doesn't see the color in my cheeks from my lies.

Sebastian strolls closer, his eyes drifting over my tight exercise gear. "Working out, huh?"

"Just a run," I reply, but I notice the heat in his eyes.

Sure enough, he pulls me into his arms, hands sliding over the curve of my ass. "I'm all sweaty," I complain, trying to pull away.

"I know."

He kisses me, slow and deep, and I can't help my body's reaction: Melting into his embrace, my lips parting to let him take his fill.

"I need a shower," I warn him breathlessly.

He smiles, devilish. "Good."

Sebastian takes me by the hand and leads me back up the stairs, straight to his bedroom—and the massive bathroom beyond. The shower there is big enough to fit an army, and Sebastian turns it on, quickly filling the marble space with hot water and steam.

"Off," he demands, nodding to my clothes. There's a

98

playful energy in the eucalyptus-scented air as I shimmy off my leggings and strip away my sports bra.

I back into the shower, naked.

"Don't take too long getting undressed," I tease him, flirty. "I might get started without you."

"We'll see about that."

Sebastian doesn't even wait to take off his clothes: he closes the distance between us, scooping me into his arms as the shower spray soaks us both.

He's still fully clothed.

"Sebastian!" I laugh in shock, but my back is already up against the marble, Sebastian's mouth on my bare neck. He kisses a blazing trail as his hands roam over my bare skin, squeezing and palming me, making me moan.

"Are you crazy?" I ask, laughing, as his clothes soak from the shower spray. "You'll ruin that suit!"

"Fuck it," Sebastian growls, devouring me.

"And there I was thinking you were going to fuck *me*..." I quip.

Sebastian pulls back, a wicked smirk on his face. "Haven't you learned yet, darling? I can multitask."

He shrugs off his soaked jacket, and yanks his belt and pants down, kicking them aside as he pushes me back against the wall again, claiming my mouth in a hot, frenzied kiss. My breath catches in my throat as his hand cups my breast, teasing my nipples, as the other hand slides between my thighs.

He groans against me. "So wet..."

"Well, we are in the shower," I reply, sassy, even as I arch against his delving fingers. Oh God, yes, *there*.

He laughs, watching me writhe. "That smart mouth of yours... I can think of a few things to do with it."

My pulse kicks.

"But I think I'll settle for it screaming my name."

Sebastian yanks off the rest of his clothes and grabs my hips. "Arms up, baby girl," he orders me, "Hold on tight."

I do as he says, wrapping my arms around his neck as he lifts my ass, spreading my legs wider. "God, I've needed this pussy," he groans, almost to himself, as the blunt head of his cock nudges at my entrance.

He sinks into me hard, thrusting me back against the slick shower wall.

I take him in with a moan, relishing the thick slide of him, how his cock stretches me wide, sending shockwaves through my entire body.

"That's right, Sparrow," Sebastian thrusts again, deeper. "Take it all." I shudder, arching up, taking in every inch until he's buried all the way to the hilt.

He nudges my chin up, so I'm trapped and gazing into his eyes. "Look at me," he demands in a rough voice. "Look at who's making you feel this good."

I want to look away. It's too intimate, too hard to block him out like this, but Sebastian is relentless, and I can't help the connection that sizzles in the air between us as our bodies move, and our eyes stay locked in a hungry, passionate stare.

Like he sees everything. Everything I am.

"*Fuck...*" We both groan together, our mouths pressed close, breath coming hot.

And then Sebastian snaps his hips back, grips my hips tighter, and fucks me hard.

I cry out in pleasure. *Yes.* He's taking exactly what he wants from me in a way that steals my breath and floods me with need. And I'm right there with him, thrusting back, arching wildly, chanting his name as I urge him on.

Deep. Deeper. *Oh.*

God, I can't enough of what he's doing to me. The way he moves against me, *inside me,* is so good that I never want it to end. But soon, too soon, my climax is cresting, and I'm clinging onto him, sobbing his name.

Just the way he wanted.

"I can feel you getting close," Sebastian pants, thrusting up inside me. "Fuck, this cunt gets so goddamn tight, it doesn't want to let me go."

"Please..." I whimper, gasping. "Oh God, don't stop!"

"Never," he vows, shifting angle so he's grinding against my clit with every thick stroke, rubbing me inside and out. It's too good, I can't take it—

"Sebastian!" I cry out, the waves of pleasure taking me over as I come with a scream. I can feel myself clamping down as he loses all control, rutting into me with a long groan until he reaches his own animal release.

Slowly, Sebastian releases me, placing me back on my feet. I steady myself with my hand on the wall since my legs feel so damn weak. Sebastian chuckles darkly and places a kiss on my forehead.

"Dirty girl."

"Good thing you're here to clean me up," I smile up at him, my mind blissfully clear, and my body humming with adrenaline. In these moments together, when the world melts away, I can forget who I am...

And why I should hate him so much.

"I wish I could stay, but I'm already running late," he says, and I swear that I can hear regret his voice. I just nod, not sure that I trust myself to speak. I might beg him to stay and pleasure me all day, to ignore the truth of our twisted relationship.

But I have a lunch to get to.

After Sebastian leaves—in another, drier bespoke suit—I luxuriate under the water for a while longer, Taking my time, slowly coming back down to earth, and trying to focus on my day ahead.

Whatever James is playing at, I need to figure him out.

Yesterday, I would have been certain I could charm the truth out of him, but now, I don't know how much of his earnest behavior was just an act.

Who is he? And more importantly, what does he want with me?

I dress carefully, in a chic, modest navy dress and designer jacket, and take a cab to the restaurant he suggested. I pause outside, surprised by the location. It's an expensive Italian place—not exactly a natural haunt for a penniless student.

"I'm meeting a friend for lunch?" I tell the hostess. "James Brooks."

She checks her book. "Ah yes, you're the first party to arrive. Please, follow me."

I make my way after her across the dining room. It's all decked out with blond wood, and white linens, and filled with snooty looking people.

Yeah, James isn't selling the post-grad researcher anymore.

I take a seat, feeling a tremor of nerves. I hate walking into a situation like this at a disadvantage, but I'm not sure what else to do. Not with the specter of those photographs hanging over me, and somebody clearly stalking my every move.

Sebastian trusts me—for now. But if he discovers that I've been lying to him...

"Ah, good, you're here."

My head jerks up at the voice, and I find myself staring at a familiar face. But it's not James sitting down opposite me.

It's Sebastian's uncle.

Richard Wolfe.

Chapter 11

Avery

I'm stunned. Of all the things I expected from this lunch, he definitely wasn't on the list.

What the hell is going on?

My eyes dart around the restaurant for a moment, looking for James as I try to figure out what's going on. Or Sebastian, about to come marching in to confront me. But they're not there. It's just Richard, who looks amused as he settles in his seat and gestures the waitress over, ordering wine and food for us both.

"... and the gnocchi, is it the black truffle in season. You like truffle, don't you?" he asks, glancing over at me with a smug grin.

He's putting on a show, I realize. Displaying just how casual and in control he is of this situation.

"The truffle sounds lovely," I reply, just as casual, even as my heart races in my chest.

Focus, I remind myself, sipping my water, trying to figure him out.

Whatever game Richard is playing, I need to be one step ahead.

"Well, this is an unexpected surprise," I tell him with a bland smile, as the waitress leaves us.

Richard gives a chuckle. "I'll bet it is. Sorry your *friend* couldn't join us, but he's served his purpose, don't you think?"

So James was a plant, after all... But I didn't see the whole picture. Richard was behind him, pulling the strings.

"And what purpose was that?" I ask brightly. "Providing some charming conversation? Setting up a few little photographs? I'm not sure what you were hoping for, but it's hardly a torrid scandal. Will this take long?" I add. "I'm due at the salon at two."

I see a flash of annoyance on Richard's face. *Aha.* He *was* hoping for more—that I would fall for James' charms, and do something incriminating.

He should have known, I'm not that easy.

"Let's not play games." Richard says abruptly, leaning forwards. "I know exactly what you're up to."

My blood runs cold.

"Well, right now I'm waiting for the breadbasket," I say, hiding my fear. I make a show of glancing around, stalling for time.

He can't know about my mission... Can he?

My mind races. I thought I'd covered my tracks. There should be no clues linking me to my former life with Nero and the Barretti organization, but if he has discovered the truth...

"Your little research project?" Richard continues.

I think of my visit to the Met Headquarters, and my fear grows. If Sebastian discovers any hint of what I'm doing to bring him down...

It's over. My vendetta will be done. Failed.

Richard smiles, watching me. He looks like a snake about to devour its prey.

"That's right." He smirks. "I know all about your secret research at the library. I already had you pegged as a common gold digger, but you've really been going the extra mile, digging into the business archives. But now... I've learned that you're looking into the accident that took my brother's life, too. So, I wonder, what's your game, Miss Carmichael?"

I pause. *Wait a minute...*

I look at the questions in his beady gaze and realize: This isn't an expose... it's a fishing expedition.

He has no idea what I'm really doing here.

Relief hits hard. I hide it, collecting myself.

"I wouldn't say I was common," I trill lightly, sipping my wine. "At least, your nephew doesn't seem to think so."

Richard snorts dismissively. "A whore in a designer dress is still just a whore."

Tell me how you really feel, why don't you?

I narrow my eyes, thoughtful. Richard clearly thinks I'm some opportunistic social climber, going after Sebastian for his money... But I can run with that. "Gold digger" is as good of a cover story as any. It's better than the truth, and besides, Richard clearly has an agenda here.

He went through the trouble of setting up the photographs, and James, and sending those threatening notes...

And he hasn't said one word to Sebastian.

This isn't about me.

The realization makes me want to laugh in relief. Of course. Richard doesn't give a damn about anyone but Richard. This is about the two of them, and whatever their power-struggle is.

I'm just a pawn, stuck in the middle.

Or at least, that's what Richard thinks.

I sit back, assessing him. He clearly wants something from me and is blind to the fact I've got my own agenda here. But that doesn't mean he's not a threat. A variable I haven't planned for. "Why should I tell you anything?" I ask, still sounding friendly.

"Because I could go to Seb with all of this." He tuts. "Now, we both know, my nephew can be a jealous, possessive man. And if he thinks you're spreading your legs all over town... That won't go well for you, I think. You'll be out of that fancy house by dinnertime, with nothing to show for all your hard work. Those long hours, I'm sure you've been putting in, making sure my nephew is... satisfied."

His eyes roam over my body, and I have to bite back a shudder of distaste.

Gross.

But if he thinks all women are scheming bitches, trading sex for status, I'm not going to argue. It's just another disguise for me.

I lean back in my chair and arch an eyebrow at Richard, summoning my best 'trophy girlfriend' vibes.

"Well, you're right," I give an exaggerated sigh. "Sebastian may be cunt-struck, but clearly, I can't fool an intelligent man like you," I add, managing to keep a straight face, even as Richard preens. "And yes, of course I've been researching the company. A woman has to do her due diligence. After all, landing a whale like Seb is no good if he's about to go down to some massive scandal. I mean, a girl must look out for her own interests, you know? I don't want my hard work to go to waste."

Richard's smile widens, clearly buying my act. "You've been thorough."

"Duh," I roll my eyes. "My friend, Kiersten? She put *years* into snaring this Greek shipping tycoon. Lost thirty pounds, waxed every last inch of her body, even learned to do, well, I won't go into it, but let's just say his tastes in the bedroom were pretty specific. Pervert. But hell, it paid off, she got the rock, the gorgeous wedding in Capri, and then, boom: Six months later, the IRS grabbed him. Confiscated all his assets! Even the smallest villa in Monaco." I sigh, shaking my head. "Now they're tied up in legal action, the divorce is taking forever... Such a waste. All her effort was for nothing."

"What a tragedy," he says dryly.

"It was!" I protest. "Look, a girl is only this young and tight for so long. I need to lock something down before I turn twenty-five, and, well, if Sebastian's a walking liability, I need to know sooner rather than later, before I've used up my best, most attractive years."

The server brings our food, and I decide to stay in character. "Umm, excuse me?" I remark, sounding bitchy. "Is this cheese?"

"Um, yes."

"I'm lactose intolerant. And I thought the vegetables would be steamed, not sautéed. Take it back."

Sorry, I sent silently, as she disappears with my food. *I'll tip, I promise.*

But clearly, my performance is convincing Richard where it counts, because he takes a bite of his food, then sits back, openly assessing me.

"You know, I have to admit that I'm rather impressed by your efforts," he says. "There are lots of women out there who are drawn to the kind of money and power our family has, but no one has gotten so close. You have some kind of hold over Sebastian, I can tell. An enterprising woman like you will go far... and even further if I help you," he adds meaningfully.

Bingo.

"How do you mean?" I sip my wine, waiting for him to reveal himself.

"Well, like I said, those photographs could be a problem for you," Richard goes on, looking smug again. "We both know they're perfectly innocent, but Sebastian might jump to the wrong conclusions. On the other hand, having an ally in the family could certainly make life easier for you. Invitations, reassurance, certain information not available to outsiders... Of course, information flows both ways."

Of course it does.

"Why would you help me?" I ask, playing dumb.

"I like your spirit," he replies. "And God knows, my nephew could use some interests outside of work. I do worry about him," he adds. "Slaving away at that company 24/7. You should help him unwind. Take a break from work more often."

Sure. So he can move in and undermine Sebastian.

"So, why don't we agree to be friends?" Richard continues, moving in for the kill. "You know, you can always come to me with anything worrying that you find about Sebastian and the business. I can help him. Protect him. And help you in the process."

I want to laugh. As if I could trust this manipulative, backstabbing bastard. I don't like the power balance between us. In this case, it skews *way* too much in his direction.

"I could do that," I say, pretending to think about it. "But reporting back to you seems so complicated. Maybe I should just go straight to Seb and tell him about this meeting. It'll surely win me his loyalty if I expose you as going behind his back like this."

Richard's smile drops. "You're playing a dangerous game, Avery. You should know by now that you need allies. After all, you've seen just what Sebastian is capable of. Your time in Larkspur was just a taste of it."

Shock makes me go rigid, and I stare at Richard with wide eyes.

"You knew I was there? Why didn't you do something?"

Richard shrugs, and I feel my stomach flip. This guy is just as bad as Sebastian.

A monster.

"It wasn't my problem, and I'm a careful man," he replies, careless. "And I'm sure it was a good lesson for you. I think you know now that Sebastian is not a man to be messed with. You would be wise to take my offer of friendship—and protection."

I don't believe for a moment that I'd be any safer allying myself with him, than going after Sebastian alone.

But Richard doesn't need to know that.

"Well, you've certainly given me a lot to think about," I say, getting to my feet. Richard looks surprised, as if he was expecting me to immediately agree to his traitorous terms.

"You're leaving already?"

"I said, I had a hair appointment. But this has been very interesting..." I give him my most charming smile. "You know, you have hidden depths, Mr. Wolfe. It's a shame Sebastian doesn't see how smart you are. He underestimates you."

I figure that blatant flattery is enough to buy me some time, and sure enough, Richard chuckles. "The same to you, my dear."

Then I waltz out—making sure to stop at the hostess stand, and leave a massive tip for our poor waitress.

Richard may not realize, but I always pay my debts.

* * *

I mull the meeting with Richard for the rest of the day. Even though he's clearly gunning for Sebastian too, I know, he can't be trusted.

The question is, how long can I play him off, acting like a gold digger—before he starts to make life difficult for me.

Because sure, right now he's just fishing for any extra intel I could throw his way about Sebastian and the business, but I know men like him. They always want more. And now that he has leverage over me, those photos and info about my daily activities...

He could be a problem. A big one.

Sebastian texts me, inviting me to dinner with some business clients, so I decide to make good on my lies: I spend the rest of the day getting my hair done and beauty treatments, as my mind works overtime, gaming out different scenarios. By the time I waltz into the cool, hip restaurant to meet Sebastian that evening, I've just about figured out my game plan.

"Hi," I greet him with a breezy kiss. "You look happy." I can tell he's in a great mood as soon as I lay eyes on him. He's got a relaxed smile on his face, and I notice the way his eyes skim down to my chest, where the V-neck of my dress shows off my cleavage.

"I'm always happy to see you," he says, drawing me closer. "Did you have a good day?"

"Mhmm," I busy myself taking a seat at the long table. His guests haven't arrived just yet, and I need to use this window. "Oh, I saw your uncle at lunch today."

My voice is casual, but Sebastian's head snaps up. "Richard?" he demands, immediately tense.

"Yup. He came by my table, sat himself down and everything." I give a little roll of my eyes.

"What did he want with you?" Sebastian looks suspicious.

I shrug. "Just small talk. He was fishing for information about you and the company, but I didn't tell him anything," I add. "He kind of gives me the creeps."

I peel off my jacket, painfully aware of Sebastian's eyes burning into me. It's a high-risk gambit, telling half-truths like this, but it's the safest option. Richard probably had someone taking photos of us together, to use as even more leverage.

I need to disarm him and pretending to come clean is the best way.

"What's wrong?" I ask, acting like I've just noticed Sebastian's mood. "Should I not have talked to him? It would have been kind of rude to ignore him, since he went out of his way to say hello. And with all those people around..."

Sebastian slowly exhales. "No, of course not. You did the right thing."

He's frowning, still distracted by the idea of Richard, so I decide to push it one step further, and try to neutralize his other big secret about me.

"You know, there's something I wanted to talk about," I say with another tentative smile. "You asked about what I wanted to do with my life now, and... Well..."

"What is it?" Sebastian looks back at me.

"I've been thinking about maybe going back to school," I announce, my heart racing. "I never got to finish college, and, I don't know, I think it would be fun to study some more. Maybe music, or history. I've been spending some time at the library, looking at different colleges and courses, seeing if it's even possible for me."

I stop, and swallow hard.

Will he buy it?

It's the most innocent explanation I can think of for the hours I've spent at the British Library. But still, it's a gamble— and could raise more questions that I don't have answers for.

"College? You never mentioned it before." Sebastian looks surprised.

I give a bashful look. "I didn't want to say anything, until I'd really thought about it. But all the choices are so overwhelming. I thought maybe you could help me decide?"

Sebastian's eyes narrow, like he's trying to figure me out, but before he can say anything, we're interrupted.

"I need to talk to you."

We both turn, and I'm shocked to see it's Becca marching towards our table. She's well put together, in the same kind of business suit I've seen her wear when she worked at Wolfe Capital, but the look in her eyes is completely different.

She's angry and maybe a little desperate.

"What are you doing here?" Sebastian asks, rising to his feet. He gestures behind her, to the staff.

"I'm the one who scheduled this dinner, remember?" Becca replies.

Sebastian gives her an icy glare. "And your presence is no longer requested. Or did the formal termination not make that clear?"

"I had no choice," she says, turning desperate. "You won't take my calls."

"I have nothing to say to you." Sebastian turns away.

"Wait, please, this is important," Becca exclaims, and I feel a pang of guilt, watching this powerful woman come unraveled right in front of me.

Because of me.

"You have to listen to me!" she continues, imploring him. "It's all a big mistake! I didn't steal from you; I never would do that. You know me! I've been loyal from the start!"

"If you're quite finished..." Sebastian says coldly. "You should leave, before you embarrass yourself any further."

There's no emotion in his voice now. Not even anger. It's somehow even worse than when he was enraged just moments ago. He's dismissive, letting her know that she means nothing to him. I can tell by the sadness on her face that she understands that just as much as I do. She knows him so well.

Becca's face slips. "Sebastian, *please!* I've been loyal to you my whole career. Why would I do this now?"

"You got greedy, I'm sure. It happens to the best of them."

The restaurant security arrives, and Sebastian nods to them. "Please escort her out."

"No!" Becca gives a wretched sob, tearing away from them. "It's not true, you have to believe me. I didn't do it!"

She turns to me then, begging silently. I look away, guilty.

"You know, I'm not sure what offends me the most," Sebastian drawls casually, giving Becca a contemptuous look. "That you had the gall to steal from me... or that you were sloppy enough to get caught. You know I demand excellence from all my employees. Clearly, you don't belong at Wolfe Capital."

He turns his back, and Becca finally admits defeat, allowing the men to lead her away.

I watch her go, gripped with guilt and shame. *I did this.* I set her up so that Sebastian would think she stole from the company and get rid of her. I thought she was the one sending me the pictures, but I was wrong.

I've ruined her life for nothing.

"Don't feel bad for her." Sebastian pulls me back to the present. "She did this to herself."

I nod, but it's clearly not convincing. "You're upset," he notes.

"I know she did a terrible thing, I just... It's a bad situation," I manage to say. "For all of you." I sigh and give him a weary smile. "I'm sorry, I'll try to be in a better mood for your clients. It's been a long day, that's all."

"It's been a long month," Sebastian replies, looking rueful. Then he pauses. "How about we take a break?"

My brow furrows. "From what?"

"London. Stress. All the drama," he says, looking determined now. "I have a place on Lake Como. We can take the jet after dinner and wake up there tomorrow morning."

"Are you serious?" I gape at him. "Just like that?"

He chuckles, amused. "Just like that. I know things can be hectic in my life, especially if you're not used to it," he adds. Sebastian takes my hand and gives it a supportive squeeze. "It'll be just the two of us, away from everything. What do you say?"

The idea is intoxicating. Escape my guilt over all my lies, and these twisted games that seem to go deeper, every day...?

Just the two of us.

"Yes," I say immediately, holding on tight to him. "Please, let's do it."

Chapter 12

Avery

I guess taking off for Lake Como for the weekend is no big deal when you're Sebastian Wolfe. After stopping back at the house after dinner to pack our bags, we head straight to the airfield, where we board a chic private jet. Just a few hours later, we arrive just outside Milan, where we spend the night at a luxurious hotel in the city.

At least, that's what I assume, when I wake alone in my private suite, with only groggy memories of the trip. I pretty much passed out the moment my head hit the buttery leather seat of the jet, so the excitement of the getaway has passed me by.

But pulling back the ornate drapes in a lavish suite, to find myself looking at gorgeous views ...

I can't help the smile of anticipation on my face.

Or the guilt I feel, over the fact I actually *wanted* to come away with Sebastian.

It makes perfect sense, I tell myself, as I get dressed for the day in jeans, and a casual cashmere sweater. This trip is perfect timing to get some distance between us and Richard's power moves. Not to mention, get Sebastian away from Becca, before she somehow gets through to him and makes him question the whole embezzlement setup.

But I know, deep down, those aren't my only reasons for saying 'Yes'. After everything I've been through over the past months, I find myself craving a break from all our twisted games. Just a couple of days to relax and refresh myself for the fights still ahead.

My anger has been corroding me from the inside out. Would it really be so bad to set it aside, and try to enjoy myself here?

There's a knock, and when I go to the door, Sebastian is waiting for me, looking deliciously dressed-down in dark-wash jeans and a cashmere sweater.

"You're awake," he says, smiling. "I thought I'd have to throw you over my shoulder and carry you to the car. Again."

I laugh. "I'm sorry! I don't know what happened, I must have been exhausted, I missed the whole flight."

"Don't apologize," Sebastian kisses my lips. "That's what we're here for."

"For me to sleep through everything?"

"To relax," he replies, and I can see, his usual tension is already gone. He almost seems content as we grab my bags, and I follow him downstairs, and out of the front of the hotel— where a classic sportscar is waiting at the curb, drawing admiring looks from people nearby.

Sebastian casually strolls over and loads our bags in the back.

"Wait, this is yours?" I ask in surprise.

"I thought we could travel in style," he replies, and I stroke the gleaming chassis reverently.

"It's a gorgeous machine," I breathe, admiring. I've always had a thing for cars, and this one is a beauty.

"I'll let you drive her later," Sebastian says, holding the passenger door open for me.

I smile. "Why is it men always think their cars are female?" I ask, teasing, as he gets settled behind the wheel.

Sebastian gives me a wicked smile. "Because the good ones are temperamental, dangerous, and give us the ride of our lives."

My laughter is swallowed up by the sound of the engine, as Sebastian guns the ignition, and roars away.

We head north of the city, along winding roads that take us into the mountains. Sebastian drives like he fucks: Hard and fast, and just like in the bedroom, I'm scared and exhilarated for the entire ride. The engine purrs and wind whips through my hair, and I have to admit, I'm having a blast, speeding through the Italian landscape, with incredible views all around. Soon, the steep hills drop away to reveal glimpses of the lake in the valley, stretching in a vivid blue pool, surrounded by the most incredible estates and villages.

Sebastian takes a sharp turn off the main road, through a wrought iron gate that swings open for us, as if by magic. He winds his way down the steep hillside towards the water along a driveway lined with tall cypress trees.

"Oh my god," I breathe, as the lake comes fully into view. It's not like any lake I know from the northeast, with rocky coves and rambling shoreline. This is grand and dramatic, edged with stone walkways and crumbling walls. The only boats I can see are sleek, old-fashioned speedboats jetting across the placid waters, and there are no rustic cabins, just massive Italian chateaus dotted along the shore.

"This is beautiful," I say, looking around, my eyes bugging

out of my head. "And it's so peaceful, too." I swear, the only sound is birdsong, and the water lapping the shore.

Sebastian smiles. "It's why I bought a place here, years ago. Just to get away from it all."

Get away from it—in total, jaw-dropping luxury.

We pull up outside the chateau, which is a gorgeous confection of faded terracotta stone, set right on the water. Everything looks historic and perfectly aging, a far cry from Sebastian's usual stark modern style.

"How old is this place?" I ask in amazement, taking in the crumbling statues dotted amongst the grounds.

"Not that old," he replies with a grin. "Five, maybe six hundred years?"

I laugh. "Practically yesterday."

"I bought it from a bankrupt Contessa," he continues, with a mischievous glint in his eye. "She demanded a night with me, in addition to the asking price."

"What?" I exclaim. "You didn't?"

Sebastian grins. "No, I didn't," he admits. "She was pushing eighty, so I just paid an extra million, instead."

I'm still laughing when an older couple emerge from the house. "Sebastian!" the woman calls, smiling. "*Ti trovo bene.*"

"Maria, *non bene come te,*" Sebastian replies, in fluent Italian. He goes to greet them, with surprising warmth.

I take them in curiously. The woman has gray hair in a long braid, and the man is wizened, with smiling eyes. They greet Sebastian enthusiastically, as if they're genuinely happy to see him.

Happy to see the big bad Wolfe?

"Avery, this is Stefano and Maria," he says, turning to me with a smile. "They live in the gatehouse here, I inherited them with the house," he adds with a wink.

Maria laughs. "He would not cope without us," she says affectionately.

"Or your cacio e pepe," Sebastian says. "I've been dreaming about it. She's an incredible cook," he tells me. "And Stefano keeps the chateau in perfect condition."

"It's nice to meet you," I say, with a little wave. Maria immediately smothers me in a hug, and kisses on both my cheeks.

"And you! Finally, he brings a girl for us to meet." She adds something in Italian, and the others laugh.

"Don't worry," Sebastian tells me. "She's just glad to have someone else to cook for. She's always worried that I'll die alone."

They laugh again, and I try to wrap my head around it: Sebastian, happy and relaxed. We really are taking a break from reality here.

Sebastian shows me to my room, which is a gorgeous suite overlooking the lake, full of stunning antique furniture and a massive four-poster bed. I freshen up, then take the long route back downstairs, exploring the house. It's like something from a magazine, but warm and lived-in, too: all the antiques and artifacts only add to its charm, with the Persian rugs, and artwork, and of course, the incredible lake views.

I find Sebastian on the terrace, pouring wine at a table set with a delicious spread of food. "A local favorite," he says, offering me a glass.

"You, or the wine?" I tease. "Maria and Stefano could lead the Sebastian Wolfe fan-club."

He smiles. "They're good people," he says, almost looking bashful. "They've been living here for years, taking care of the place."

"And you," I comment, taking in the lunch spread. "This all looks amazing."

We sit down and fill our plates. There are cold cuts of salami and prosciutto, cheeses, fresh ciabatta, and salad with a delicious dressing. I find myself ravenous, and happily try bites of everything. It's cool out, but the sun is shining off the water, and I take a deep breath of the clean air, relaxing more with every minute.

"What's on your mind?" Sebastian asks. He sits back, watching me.

"I was just thinking, this is like a whole different world," I confide. "I already feel like London is a different lifetime."

"Good," Sebastian says. "You deserve a real holiday."

The subtext is lingering just beneath the surface. *Because of everything he put me through.* But I push it back and take a sip of wine instead.

It's too beautiful, and the food is too good, to ruin with that bitter truth.

"So, Maria made it seem like you don't bring guests here..." I say, changing the subject. I give him a curious look. "Seems like the perfect party house to me. There's not a woman alive who wouldn't swoon over this view."

Sebastian smiles at me. "And are you? Swooning?"

"Well, this bread is making me weak at the knees, that's for sure," I tease back.

He laughs, and suddenly pulls me into his lap. I squeal, as he buries a kiss against my neck. "Can we make a deal?" he asks, resting his chin on my shoulder. "Can we pretend like the outside world doesn't exist? It's just us for the weekend," he adds. "You and me, right here."

I turn to look at him, surprised by the sincerity in his voice —and the expression of hope I see in his eyes.

Something twists behind my ribcage. Something that feels an awful lot like happiness.

"You read my mind," I tell him quietly, kissing him on the cheek. "Just you and me. It's a deal."

After our lunch, we take a water taxi across the lake to Cernobbio, a small town with classic Italian architecture and a historic town square. It's busy with tourists strolling the winding, cobbled streets, and we have fun just exploring, taking in the street vendors and gorgeous views. Sebastian holds my hand, and it's easy to pretend we're just like the other couples and honeymooning newlyweds posing for photos by the shore.

"What do you say to some gelato?" he suggests, nodding to a little store with a line out the door. "This place is a local legend."

"Obviously. I'm shocked it took you this long," I laugh. "Isn't it like a local law, you have to eat it three times a day?"

"You're right, we should catch up, immediately," Sebastian grins.

Then his phone sounds, in his pocket. He pauses.

"Ignore it," I urge, "Didn't you say the real world doesn't exist?"

"I know, but..." Sebastian pulls it out, and checks the screen. His smile drops. "I have to take this. Are you OK amusing yourself for a couple of hours?"

"Sure," I reply, trying to ignore my disappointment. "I'm happy just walking around."

"I think we can do better than that," Sebastian says, giving me a smirk—and his black Amex card. "See you at Harry's Bar, on the harbor, at four?"

"See you then," I agree. "I'll be the one with all the shopping bags."

He chuckles, dropping a kiss on my forehead before strolling away, already with his focused expression on as he pulls out his phone.

I wonder what's so important that it's interrupting our weekend. I hope it's nothing I need to know; even if Sebastian has to get back to reality briefly, I want to maintain the illusion that I have absolutely no cares in the world.

Something tells me, I won't get the chance again.

So, I dedicate myself to the vacation vibe: I buy myself a delicious cone of hazelnut gelato and stroll the waterfront until I see a pretty bag in a boutique window. Then I set about giving the black Amex a workout for the rest of the afternoon, on clothing, shoes, and all that fine Italian craftsmanship. I'm just emerging from yet another boutique, when my own phone buzzes with a text.

Relax with Stonebridge Spa this weekend. We have new treatments: Call to book now.

It's from Charlie—and she's using the same code as before about the spa. Smart. If Sebastian glances at my phone, he'd have no idea she contacted me.

'New treatments'... that must mean she has information for me. And 'book now' means she wants to arrange to meet.

I pause. I should find a quiet spot and call her right away, but instead, I tuck my phone away. I feel guilty for not responding immediately, especially since I have so much at stake, but I *did* promise to forget about the outside world for a while.

And London feels like a long way away.

It's almost four, so I head to meet Sebastian at the bar he mentioned, right on the waterfront. It's a cute spot, with tables outside under a striped awning, and I can spot Sebastian sitting at a table, drinking a beer.

And he's not alone.

There's a beautiful woman sitting beside him, a brunette wearing big sunglasses, and that effortless European chic style. They're talking and laughing together, totally at ease. And as I watch, she leans over and squeezes Sebastian's arm, her touch lingering.

It's clear they know each other. Very well.

Chapter 13

Sebastian

"So, this is the woman who's making you so happy..." Bianca remarks, watching Avery approach us across the square. "I can see why."

I rise to my feet as Avery arrives, laden down with shopping bags. "I see you've been busy," I tell her, and her eyes flick back and forth between me and Bianca.

"You too," she says, and although she's smiling, I can see there's tension in her eyes as she takes in the other woman at the table.

Is she... jealous?

"This is Bianca," I introduce them. "She's an old friend of mine from England. She lives here now."

"Great to meet you," Avery says, still wary.

I hide a grin. Avery drives me crazy when she so much as looks at another man, so I have to admit, it's rather nice to have the tables turned. To see she cares enough to be jealous of another woman.

Not that she has anything to worry about in that department. I haven't so much as felt a flicker of desire for another woman since Avery came into my life. My attention is solely on her—for better or worse.

She's the only one I crave to possess, body and soul.

"Well, I'm afraid I have to get back," Bianca says, rising to her feet. "We're having people over tonight. Are you sure you won't join us for dinner, Seb? I'd love to get to know Avery better," she adds with a smile. "He's barely said a word about you," she tells Avery, rolling her eyes. "Men, they're more than happy to share every detail of their new business acquisition, but when it comes to the more important things in life? Not a whisper."

I smile. "I'm not sure, we only arrived this morning—"

"Nonsense," Bianca talks over me. "You will both come and have a marvelous time. I won't hear any excuses."

I chuckle. "Well, in that case... We'll be there."

"Perfecto," she announces, kissing me on both cheeks. "Bring some of that fabulous wine you have gathering dust in your cellar. Avery, lovely to meet you, don't let him change his mind!"

Bianca waltzes away.

I sit back, smiling, but Avery is watching her go, furrowing her brow. "She seems nice," she says blandly.

God, she's adorable like this.

"You're jealous," I say, amused.

"Should I be?" Avery arches an eyebrow at me, challenging.

"Not at all." I take a drink. "Bianca is an old friend of mine. A married friend," I add. "She and her wife, Violetta, live up in the hills near my estate here."

"Her wife..." Avery echoes. Then she blushes. "Oh."

"Exactly." I drop my voice, and lean closer. "Do you really think another woman could compare to you?" I murmur, tracing my fingertips along her bare arm. "You're the only one I want, Sparrow. In every possible way."

Avery's cheeks flush, and her lips part, tantalizing.

"I want you on your knees, those pretty lips wide open for me, begging for my cock," I murmur, my voice turning rough as I see how she responds to my words. "I want you tied to that bed of yours, mine to worship as I see fit. Your tight cunt clenching around me, your body arched and ready to break."

Avery shivers, swaying closer. Fuck, her desire is written right there on her face, glazed and wanting. "You'd like that, wouldn't you?" I growl, "My good girl. You'll be weak from fucking me, a sweaty, dripping mess, so used you don't know whether to beg me to stop, or plead for another goddamn inch."

She exhales in rush. "*Sebastian...*"

"I know, baby. You're wet right now, just thinking about it."

Silently, she meets my eyes, and nods.

Goddamn.

I bolt to my feet and throw down a hundred euro note. Drinks can wait. Right now, I need to be inside this girl, making her scream my name.

I practically drag Avery to the water taxi, and back to the villa.

The whole way there, I can't keep my hands to myself. I slide a hand up her thigh and play with the ends of her hair as we speed across the lake. I trace her spine with the palm of my hand and knead her ass, not caring that the driver can see us from where we're sitting.

Let him see that she's mine.

Let them all fucking see.

And Avery loves it. I can tell from the excitement in her eyes, and the way her breath catches with every illicit touch. It turns her on, to be displayed like this, her desire on show to the world as I stake my claim.

Mine.

Back at the villa, I'm on her like an animal. Kissing, touch-

ing, needing to feel every inch of her body. An animal possession is rising in me, something so primal I can't hold back.

"On the bed," I growl—and then I don't wait before tossing
her down, stripping her clothes from her body until she's
laying, naked and spread for me.

"Fuck, this pussy..." I groan, gripping her thighs and parting
them wider, seeing how she clenches for me, already soaking
wet with her own desire. Lust strikes, hot and wild. "You know,
men start wars for pussy like this," I tell her, bending over her,
nipping at one bare thigh. "They fight to the death, just for a
single taste of this sweetness. Burn whole fucking empires to
the ground."

I bury my face between her legs, loving the sound of her
screams as I wrap my lips around that tight little bud and suck.
Hard.

"Oh my God!" Avery's legs clamp around my head, her
body arching off the bed in shock. "Sebastian!"

"That's right, Sparrow," I growl, lapping at her wetness like
a man possessed. Because I am. This girl has put a fucking spell
on me, and whether it's a curse, or a blessing, I still don't know.

All I know is that I was made to claim her, with my mouth,
my hands...

My aching cock.

Slipping two fingers inside, I get her ready to take me. She's
still so fucking tight, so new to this, so I press my tongue against
her clit as I pump my fingers deeper, making her writhe and
moan as I stretch her open.

"There, *fuck*, don't stop!" she cries, clutching the sheets.

I growl into her. Stop? I couldn't tear myself away from this
feast if there were a hundred men beating down the door. I'm
drunk on her, devouring every drop until her whole body goes
tense—and then shatters, coming in a rush of wetness with my
name on her lips.

I rise to my feet and strip off the rest of my clothes, watching her body heave and gasp with the force of her climax.

Good. She's nice and warmed up for me now, because fuck, I won't go easy on her.

I position myself between her legs, grab her hips, and bury myself to the hilt.

Fuck.

It's too good, the feel of her, so tight and slick around my cock. I piston deeper, and she moans, clenching hard, making me roar with the pleasure.

Every time. Every goddamn time. I lose my mind over this woman.

I lose *myself* in her sweet cunt.

"So tight for me, baby," I growl, slamming into her. "Who owns this pussy? Who do you belong to?"

"You!" Avery cries out, so sweetly. "It's yours. Fuck. Yes!"

Her whole body is shaking with the impact of my thrusts. She's writhing, arching, trying to get purchase as I drive into her relentlessly.

Goddamn, there's nothing sweeter.

I scoop her up and roll us, so she's on top. I bring her down hard on my lap, impaling her with my cock.

"Oh my god!" Avery throws her head back as I grind up into her, adjusting to the new angle, so fucking deep, her body is swallowing me whole.

"Ride me," I command her roughly. "Ride my fucking cock."

Her eyes widen, and even through the haze of her lust, I see the inexperience written on her face. "Take your pleasure," I urge her on, gripping her hips, and starting to move her. "Move, fuck, just like that."

She starts to ride, tentative, then stronger as she finds the right spots, her pussy clenching around me like a goddamn vice.

Fuck yes.

"That's right, baby, milk my cock." I groan, watching her grow braver with every thrust, until she's bouncing on my dick with total abandon, sweet tits jiggling, flushed and panting with her own pleasure. "Are you going to be my good girl?" I demand, landing a stinging slap on her ass. "Are you going to take every goddamn drop?"

"Yes!" she cries, moving faster. Frenzied and wild. "Oh god, yes!"

I reach up and grip her breasts, pinching her stiff nipples, loving how her eyes roll back and her cries grow more fevered as our bodies slam together. I spank her again, and she wails, grinding at me, chasing her release.

She's a fucking work of art. A masterpiece of my own creation.

And I've barely started training her yet.

I roar, thrusting up into her, grabbing her wrists with one hand and gripping them tightly behind her back, pinning her in place. She's still on top of me, but I'm the one setting the pace now, slamming her body down on my cock over and over as her scream reach a fever pitch.

"Look at me while I'm fucking you," I command her, grabbing her by the throat.

Avery's eyes flash open, glazed in lust, so out of her mind I feel my balls tighten up right then and there.

"Look at the man who's branding your body," I squeeze her throat tighter, watching the rush of shock—and pleasure in her gaze. "You love it, don't you baby? Your life in my hands. My good little whore."

I slam up into her tight cunt again, holding her totally at my mercy. Avery's eyes roll back. "Yes!" she screams, her body going limp in total surrender. "I love it, oh God, *Sebastian —Seb, OH!*"

Her orgasm hits like a goddamn tidal wave, and I feel her whole body spasm around my cock, like she's trying to kill me with the overwhelming perfection of it all.

Still, I don't stop.

I roll us again, so she's on her back, and bury myself balls-deep with a roar. Over and over, I slam into her, something snapping inside me, my last vestige of self-control. I don't give it to her slowly or make it sweet.

I fuck her, brutal and rough, right the way through the shudders of her first climax...

... and screaming into her next.

"Mine," I growl, frenzied, as the red haze rises, blotting out everything but the tight clench of her cunt and the look of total submission in her eyes. "Only mine..."

I don't even hear her sobbed response as I slam into her deep, and grind, *fuck*, as the tension unlocks in my spine and I explode, unleashing my seed inside her with a furious howl.

Fuuuuck.

After the tension leaves me, I lay back, watching as Avery comes back down to earth. As usual, a flash of panic skitters across her face, as she remembers just what she did.

And with whom.

One of these days, I swear, I'll banish that expression for good, leaving nothing but lazy satisfaction in its place.

She modestly brings the sheets around her. "I'm going to go take a shower," she says, flushed and gorgeous.

I'm tempted to join her, and fuck her right into another screaming orgasm, but my cellphone buzzes on the desk.

"Go ahead," I tell her, lazily getting to my feet—and sending her back to her room with a slap on her bare ass. "I'll see you downstairs, and we can head to dinner."

"Don't think I'm not keeping score," she tells me playfully from the doorway.

"Of your orgasms?"

"No," she grins. "Your work calls. We had a deal, remember?"

I wince. "I know. But some things can't wait."

She leaves me in peace, and I reluctantly answer the call. I should have known my plan to leave London behind wouldn't last for long.

When you're running an empire like mine, there's always something demanding attention.

"What?" I bark, answering. It's one of my executives, sounding nervous. As he should. "This better be important."

"I'm sorry," he blurts. "It's just... You said you wanted to hear it in person. When the Dunleavey deal closed."

I exhale, relaxing. "It's all finalized?"

"Yes, the lawyers just signed off. It's done."

"Good."

I told them to fast-track everything, but still, it's moved faster than I anticipated. The old man didn't put up much of a fight, which surprises me, considering how important it was to him that the company remain a family business.

He probably knows better than to delay the inevitable. Plus, I added a few sweeteners to the deal, which means none of his board would stand in my way.

"Should we move ahead to phase B?" my exec asks, eager. "We can get the announcement about the layoffs out first thing Monday."

Ah yes, the layoffs. I always knew I'd be stripping Dunleavey for parts. The company has valuable dockside real estate, and an excellent transport network, and nothing much else besides. I've already got a dozen hungry bidders for the raw components, and the workforce isn't part of the deal.

Still, I find myself pausing. Avery was furious when she'd heard my plans. *'Those are people's lives,'* she'd said angrily. *'How can you treat them like that?'*

"Is there a change of plans?" my exec asks, reading into my silence. "I thought this was what you wanted."

"It was. It is," I correct myself, pushing aside the unwelcome sense of guilt. "Go ahead with the schedule. And don't disturb me again."

I hang up, rattled. I don't think twice when it comes to my business decisions, and certainly not out of some misplaced sense of loyalty. The bottom line is all that counts.

So why the hesitation this time?

Avery.

The answer is down the hallway, singing in the shower. Her voice drifts out on the evening breeze, lilting and sweet.

Almost like love...

I tense, shocked by the thought. She's gotten under my skin. Avery is an obsession, to be sure, but is there more to it than that?

I think about the way it feels to watch her light up—over a beautiful view, or a fine meal, or just a word of praise. How her happiness is addictive to me, and her pleasure even more of a prize.

The fact that I'm willing to kill anyone that would hurt her.

I stand in the hallway, watching her through her open bedroom door. She strolls across the room, dressed only in a towel. Her hair wet, her lips still humming that song. She pauses over outfit choices, and I can see the decision weigh on her. Wanting to look good for me.

Wanting to please me.

I feel the strangest jolt of longing in my chest. Because I know I'm not worthy of this care and careful consideration.

That light of hers that's shining through is too good for a monster like me.

I don't deserve her. And once she learns the truth about me, she'll know it too.

But since when did I ever accept what I deserve?

I take what I want, without mercy. And if the most I can hope for is to steal just a few more days with her, then fuck, I'll savor every second.

But still, a voice whispers inside me, a couple of days will never be enough. I need more than the weekend. More than even a few months...

I want her mine *forever*.

Chapter 14

Avery

Bianca's home is up in the hills, a breathtaking old farmhouse-style chateau with sweeping views of the lake, surrounding by Cypress trees and pretty gardens.

"It's so beautiful here," I take it all in, as Sebastian leads us through the open doors, and into an airy foyer, with old terra-cotta tiles underfoot.

"Violetta is a designer," he explains. "The house has been featured in several magazines."

I can see why. Everything is stripped back and minimal, but instead of feeling stark or cold, there's a luxurious, rustic vibe: soft limewash on the stucco walls, oversized couches upholstered in white linen, and occasional accent pieces in raw, aged wood. I see a huge farmhouse kitchen and a cozy library, before Sebastian takes us through and out of the back doors, which have been flung wide open to the beautiful terrace, where a small group is already gathered, sipping wine and browsing appetizers.

A long table is set for dinner, with beautiful flowers and

ceramics, and there are lights on strings hanging over the table and casting a golden glow over everything as the sun makes its descent in the sky. When I take in the other guests, I feel relief that I picked a simple navy shift dress, and low-heeled boots: The vibe is casual and eclectic. There's a mix of guests of all ages, and while everyone seems effortlessly stylish, it's a low-key kind of look, not the dressed-up society scene like back in London.

"Darling!" A gorgeous Italian woman with long black hair and layers of beaded jewelry approaches us, her arms held out to Sebastian. "I was worried you wouldn't come."

"Violetta, when have I ever let you down?" he asks, bending down to greet her. "You know Bianca would never let me hear the end of it."

"She is persuasive," Violetta says with an affectionate smile. "And you must be the lovely Avery," Violetta turns, smothering me in a hug and air kisses before I can even reply. "We are so happy to meet you. You know, he never brings his women to the lake. We are all dying to discover your secrets."

I give a nervous laugh. "No secrets here," I say quickly.

She just grins. "Nonsense. Anyone who can tame the big, bad Wolfe is a woman we want to know."

"Hey," Sebastian protests, but with a smile.

"You call him that, too?" I ask in disbelief. I would have thought Sebastian would destroy anyone who dared tease him with his nickname.

"But of course," Violetta exclaims. "Especially when it annoys him."

"You could never annoy me," Seb says smoothly, giving me a wink. "You merely build my character."

Violetta hoots with laughter, then links her arm through mine. "Go shoo, help Bianca with something," she orders him. "I'm going to get to know your lovely girlfriend."

Sebastian smirks. "Good luck," he says to me. "Let me know when you need rescuing."

"Hush, you." Violetta pouts, "Avery and I will be the best of friends."

She steers me off, puts a wineglass in my hand, and then proceeds to introduce me to all the other guests. My mind is reeling just trying to keep track, but everyone seems so friendly and down-to-earth: there's an artist, a human rights lawyer, a food historian who runs trips foraging in the Italian country-side... I ask a million questions, and by the time I rejoin Sebastian and we sit down to dinner, I'm starting to relax and have a good time.

"How are you holding up?" he asks casually, draping an arm over the back of my chair. Sebastian is completely at ease, talking knowledgeably, but also just sitting back and enjoying the dinner. He clearly knows just about everyone here, and these aren't the obscenely wealthy jetsetters that I expect him to spend time with.

They're all surprisingly... nice.

And Sebastian is acting so friendly, too, I'm getting whiplash again. Does he turn into a different person, the moment we arrive in Italian airspace?

"Now, tell us about you, Avery," Bianca fixes me with a curious look. "What is your story?'

"No story," I say with a bland smile.

At least, not one that I'm about to broadcast to this table.

"But how did you meet Seb?" Violetta pitches in. "Have you been seeing each other long?"

"Easy with the inquisition," Sebastian speaks up.

"But we're just dying to know all the juicy details," Violetta pouts.

He chuckles. "No juice. Avery and I met in Cannes," he adds, giving me a private smile. "A couple of months ago. And if you want to know more than that... Well, I'll need some of your famous tiramisu to loosen my tongue."

"You're no fun!" Bianca protests, laughing, but Sebastian's evasion works, and the conversation moves on.

When the main course is finished, and Bianca clears some plates, making room for dessert, I bob up and volunteer to help. I want to find out more about this alter-ego Sebastian has been hiding. The one who cracks jokes, and smiles, so relaxed, as the dusk turns to nightfall.

I follow her inside, to the kitchen.

"I hope we're not overwhelming you with questions," Bianca says, friendly as she bustles around. "I'm just so happy to see Sebastian this way."

"So, you know he's not like this all the time?" I venture.

She laughs. "I do. You know, he likes to keep up appearances as the Master of the Universe, but there's so much more to him than that. I keep telling him it's not a crime to be engaged with the world, to care about these causes, and do good work, but he insists on keeping his cutthroat reputation." She rolls her eyes affectionately. "As if his empire would crumble, if his foundation became public knowledge."

Foundation? It's news to me, and I'm about to ask more, when Sebastian strolls in, carrying some empty dishes.

"Tell him, Avery," Bianca adds, giving Sebastian a teasing grin. "Doing good is not a crime."

"But then people wouldn't quake from the big bad Wolfe," Sebastian says, teasing.

Bianca rolls her eyes.

"What foundation?" I venture.

"Seb's, of course," Bianca says. "Don't tell me you've been keeping it from her, too? Honestly," she says, shaking her head at me. "If I'd spent hundreds of millions on charity projects, the way he has, I'd be singing it from the rooftops."

"I'm not the story here," Sebastian says with a shrug. "And technically, you're the one doing the spending. I count on you to do good in my name."

Bianca laughs. "And I enjoy every dollar of it!"

She takes dessert out, but I pause in the kitchen with Sebastian. "I didn't know you were involved with charity," I say, frowning. How does this fit in with Sebastian's heartless attitude?

"I told you, it was my father's thing. I just... expanded it, that's all," he replies. "Bianca is the director, she's the one who's really the engine behind the giving program. I just write the checks."

"The checks that make it all possible." I recall a conversation from dinner just moments before, when Bianca detailed a program she was running to provide education to girls in third-world countries.

That was possible because of Sebastian?

But he seems uncomfortable claiming any credit, and directs us back to the dinner table, where dessert is served. Several people have switched seats, to talk to new people, and I watch Sebastian talk and laugh with new eyes, noting the clear closeness he has with Bianca.

I wonder what the story is there...

"You are not hungry?" Violetta perches in the chair beside me, eyeing my untouched flan.

I quickly pick up my spoon. "Oh no, it's delicious."

Across the table, Bianca says something, and Sebastian laughs loudly.

Violetta follows my gaze. "It's good to see him so happy. I'm sure you are to credit for that."

"He and Bianca seem close," I say carefully.

Violetta nods, still smiling. "You know about the crash, of course?" she asks.

Wait, what?

I nod, keeping my expression neutral, even as my mind races.

Violetta continues, not knowing I'm in the dark. "The accident was hard for them," she says. "Both of them losing their fathers like that in one night, so young. But Sebastian reached out to Bianca when it was over, and that's what brought them together, connected in their grief."

Holy shit!

I try not to show my shock as her words sink in.

Bianca's father was killed in the crash, too?

I remember mentions of another vehicle, the one Patrick Wolfe hit head-on, but I've never seen any details of the death. I'd assumed everyone in the second car was fine.

Why wasn't this headline news?

"He's been so supportive," Violetta continues, oblivious. "Like a brother. He's always been there for her, he even funded her education and study abroad here in Italy. I have to thank him for that too," she adds with a smile. "Since it's how we met. And now, she's so happy, running the foundation, making such an impact, in memory of the ones they've lost. We are very lucky to have him as a part of our lives."

"That's... amazing," I say faintly.

And it is. I'm learning so much new information about Sebastian tonight, and I watch him carefully for the rest of the evening, until at last, people begin to say their goodbyes and leave. Bianca and Violetta show us to the door, urging Sebastian to extend his trip. "Or at least, come back soon," Bianca insists. "You too, Avery."

Sebastian just smiles. "We'll see."

Bianca pauses, her hand on his arm. "And I meant what I said." She tells him cryptically. "You should call me if it gets too hard, this year."

I wonder what she means, but Sebastian doesn't explain, and I don't want to pry. Besides, I already have enough to process, as we drive the winding hillside road back down to his place by the water.

"I had fun tonight," I venture, as Sebastian opens the car door and helps me out. "Your friends are lovely."

He smiles at me, smoldering. "Not as lovely as you..."

He kisses me, soft and surprisingly tender. I sway into his embrace, my confusion melting away the moment he touches me.

Whoever Sebastian is with his friends and family, I know who he is when I'm in his arms.

Sensual. Masterful. *Mine.*

He pulls back and takes me by the hand, leading me through the dark, empty house and up to his bedroom. Moonlight shines through the open drapes, reflecting off the lake outside, and there's a hushed feeling in the air between us now. A quiet intensity in every glance and touch.

We don't speak, as Sebastian pulls me into his arms again. Somehow, it feels like words aren't necessary as he unzips the back of my dress, letting it fall to the floor at my feet.

I step out of my boots, kicking them to the side as I move to unbutton his shirt. The second his bare skin is exposed, I'm running my hands over his chest and tracing the lines of his torso, reveling in the feel of him, and the way he inhales a sharp breath at my touch.

Sebastian dips his head and kisses along the side of my neck, making me shudder. He unhooks my bra, freeing my breasts, and then he's on his knees, lavishing me with his tongue.

"*Oh...*" My moan echoes in the darkness, and I bury my hands in his hair, holding him to me as I whimper. He takes my nipple into his mouth, each dragging pull of his mouth sending waves of pleasure through me, all the way to my core.

As if he knows just how much I want him, Sebastian hooks his fingers under the sides of my panties and slides them down my shaking thighs. He breathes against me, hot, as I quiver.

"Sebastian..."

He licks up against me, hot and determined, and I gasp, clinging to his shoulders for balance as he teases my clit with gentle laps, driving me crazy, until I'm aching for more.

Bold, I take his chin, and tilt his face up to me. "I need you," I say urgently. "Please, I need you inside..."

Lust flashes across his face, and he rises to his feet, stripping off the rest of his clothes as he steers us to the bed. I touch him greedily, running my hands over his chest, and fisting his hard cock in my hand, feeling it leap and stiffen even more.

God, I want this.

I lay back, already parting my thighs for him. Inviting him inside, where I crave his thick length the most. But instead of laying down with me, Sebastian pulls me closer to where he's standing at the edge of the bed. He lifts my legs, resting them on each shoulder, and lines his cock up at my entrance.

He pushes into me slowly, *god, so slow.*

And fuck, it doesn't end.

"Avery..." he groans, and I arch up towards him with an answering moan, already blissful from this new angle. He's sinking into me deeper than ever before, stretching me open, his cock filling me to the brim.

But he's not rough or demanding. Not this time. Sebastian's eyes lock on mine, glittering with intensity in the darkness, as he slowly pumps into me, grinding just right, every inch sparking new friction and sensation that seems amplified by the hush all around us, and the distant sound of the lake lapping below.

Oh god.

I moan again, feeling my pleasure build with the tender intensity. My orgasm is right there, lingering just beneath the surface.

"Sebastian," I whimper, clutching at him. "Don't stop..."

"Never," he vows, keeping up his hypnotic rhythm. "I'll get you there, Sparrow. Every fucking time."

His hand moves between us, finding the tight bud of my clit, and stroking it softly, timed with every slow thrust.

Fuck.

It's incredible, not just the pleasure building, tightening in my entire body, but the connection between us, electric in the night air. The outside world disappears, and our eyes are locked, and our bodies feel perfectly in sync, as I rise to meet every sinuous grind of his hips, his cock stroking my most tender spots. He reads me perfectly, knowing just the right pace to make me crazy, the angle that sends my body soaring to the edge.

This is all that matters. This is all I need.

I try to delay my climax, to savor this heady bliss, but Sebastian's strokes are too intoxicating, the delicious friction he's wreaking on my body. His caress stays, so steady, matching every stroke until I can't keep the waves at bay.

My climax shatters through me, my moans of pleasure echoing into the night as Sebastian pumps again, twice more, and shudders above me, sounding his own orgasm with a groan of release as he collapses forwards, covering my naked body with his own.

I lay there, my arms around him, feeling the race of both our heartbeats, and the sweet warmth of adrenaline racing in my veins.

Who is this man?

The question pierces my afterglow, even as I hold him tightly.

All my research has never hinted at this part of Sebastian's life I'm seeing on this trip: The good that he's done. The friendships he's made. The people who genuinely love and support him.

I almost can't process the switch. I've only seen his ruthless, heartless side. The man who'll stop at nothing to get what he wants—and hurt whoever is standing in his way. But now, learning about the projects and people he's been hiding...

Now I wonder if I've ever really known him at all.

Chapter 15

Avery

S omething's changed.

When I woke in the morning after Bianca's dinner party, all the closeness and intimacy Sebastian had shared the night before was gone. Out of nowhere, he was closed off again. Cool and reserved.

"I have business back in London," was all he said, barely looking up from his phone. So, just like that, we packed and flew back early. Now, we're in the car driving back from the airfield, and I still can't figure out what's going on.

But from the tense vibes that Sebastian is radiating in my direction, it's clear our brief vacation from reality is over, and we're back to secrets and suspicion again.

"It looks like it's going to rain today," I say blandly, looking out at the cloudy London skies. The weather is a lame attempt to start a conversation, but I don't know what else to say.

'What's wrong?' 'Why have you shut me out all over again?' 'I like the man I saw in Italy, what happened to him?'

But I can't ask those questions, and Sebastian keeps scrolling on his phone. Too soon, we're pulling down his street.

"Do you have to get straight to the office?" I ask.

He nods. "Work is crazy. I don't know when I'll be home."

"Maybe we could make reservations, for a late dinner?" I suggest, trying again. "Not Italian though," I crack. "I'm not sure anything could live up to Bianca's cooking. She's ruined me for all Italian restaurants here in town."

I smile at him, friendly. Sebastian's expression remains stony.

"I told you, I have to work late," he says, sounding impatient. "Order whatever you like for dinner. Don't wait up for me."

The car comes to a stop, and he looks at me expectantly. "Oh," I swallow hard, realizing he's waiting for me to get out and leave him. "You're going straight in? Don't you want to shower and change first?"

"I can do that at the office."

"Right. Of course," I reply quietly. "Have a good day, then."

I get out of the car, and the driver brings around my bags, before driving away again. I watch the car go, feeling totally confused.

Did I do something wrong?

"Welcome home."

I spin around. It's the house manager, waiting patiently on the front steps. "Leon, hi, you startled me."

"Good trip?" he asks, as he takes my bags in.

"Great," I say brightly. And it isn't even a lie. Everything save the past four hours as blissful.

It's just the present, right now, that's confusing me so much.

"Do you want lunch?" he asks. "I can fix something."

I shake my head. "Thanks, but I've been cooped up all morning with travel. I think I'll take a run and stretch my legs."

"Suit yourself," he gives a shrug, and disappears back

towards the kitchen – where I'm pretty sure I can hear some kind of sports playing on the TV.

At least he knows how to entertain himself, waiting around for Sebastian to arrive home. Me? I should be used to it by now, but as I change into some workout gear, and hit the road, my sneakers pounding the pavements, I realize, I'm feeling strangely at a loss.

I thought something had really changed between us.

I run harder, pushing my body, as my mind struggles to process everything that's happened over the past few days. I really thought I'd seen a glimpse of the real Sebastian in Italy, that there was more to him than the cold, heartless monster I'd taken him to be.

He was warmer. Relaxed. Kind-hearted. The kind of man I could actually care about. And meeting Bianca and his other friends, I really saw a different side to him. Felt a difference in the way he looked at me, how he made love to me.

At least, I thought I did.

But now... I don't know what happened, or where I stand.

I pause for breath, panting. Maybe Sebastian is just stressed by some emergency at the office. Maybe this has no connection to the two of us.

I pull out my phone and write a text to him before I can change my mind.

This weekend... do you want to go back to that club?

I hit 'send', biting my lip. It's a cheap shot, sure, using the reminder of our sexy adventures to get a response from him, but what can I say?

I'm prepared to play dirty.

I see the three little dots on the screen that indicate he's working on a response, and I feel my anticipation grow.

Then, the dots disappear.

Nothing.

I exhale in a rush, suddenly feeling like the biggest fool.

What the hell are you doing? I scold myself, tucking my phone away. Hanging out, waiting for a text like he's my high school sweetheart, or new boyfriend?

One weekend shouldn't make a difference. And it doesn't, I tell myself firmly. *It can't.* Just because Sebastian throws a couple of hundred million pounds at good causes and has managed to make a few genuine friends along the way, it doesn't wipe his slate clean.

He's still the man that wreaks havoc, leaving damaged lives, and ruined people in his wake.

He's still my enemy, the man I've sworn to destroy.

But still, even my familiar refrain doesn't ring quite so true anymore. I sigh, turning to walk back the way I came. I'm supposed to hate the man. But it turns out, hate was so much easier than this blur of desire and resentment, affection and bitterness.

I just don't know which way the scales are going to tip next.

I return home, determined not to let Sebastian's distant behavior affect me anymore. I shower and eat a light dinner, watching some TV to pass the time, until finally, I turn in for bed.

But I can't sleep. I lay there in the dark, willing myself to stop thinking about Sebastian, but a part of me stays alert, listening for the door, until finally, I hear movement downstairs.

I check my phone. It's gone one in the morning.

Is he trying to avoid seeing me?

What if I'd been waiting up for him?

I spring out of bed, and grab my robe, all my frustration and self-loathing boiling over in my veins. I march downstairs and find him in his office. He has his back turned to me, and he's pouring a drink.

"Nice of you to come home," I say icily.

"Go away, Avery," he says without even turning to face me. That just makes me angrier.

"What the hell is wrong with you?" I demand, hating myself for feeling so rejected. "Did you use up your annual allocation of being a nice person in Italy, and now we're back to you acting like you don't give a fuck?"

Sebastian finally turns. His tie is undone, and his shirt-sleeves are pushed up. "I'm not in the mood for this," he says, his voice low and dangerous—and just a little slurred.

He's drunk.

I blink in shock as he takes a swig of whisky, straight from the bottle. I've never seen him like this before. Sebastian Wolfe is the master of control. He's never sloppy. Never has one too many.

Except tonight.

I take a half-step closer, confused.

"No." Sebastian holds up a hand. "Don't. I mean it, Avery. Go back to bed and leave me be... If you know what's good for you."

There's a dangerous edge in his expression, but it doesn't scare me. Nor does his veiled warning.

If I knew what was good for me, I would never have started on this mission of revenge in the first place.

"That's not how this works, not anymore," I snap back. "You can't just order me around, without any explanation. Like it or not, we're in a relationship here," I add, advancing closer. "And that means you need to treat me like a person, and not some toy you can pick up and put down when it amuses you."

"I needed my space."

"Why?' I demand, moving closer. "After everything we shared in Italy, why are you suddenly pushing me away?"

"I can't do this," Sebastian takes another gulp of whiskey. "Not today."

"What's so special about today?" I shoot back at him, and he looks over at me, his eyes like bottomless pools of darkness.

"It's the anniversary of my father's death."

Fuck.

I stand there—and my heart aches for him. "Oh, Sebastian," I say, reaching out to hold him. "I'm so sorry—"

"Goddamn it, Avery!" Sebastian suddenly roars, eyes flashing. "Why are you even still here? You should have left when you had the chance!"

I gape, shocked, as Sebastian paces angrily. "Just say what you're thinking," he adds bitterly. "I'm a fucking monster, and we both know there's no chance of redeeming me, so what the hell are you sticking around for? I don't deserve even a second of your time!"

He hurls the bottle to the ground, and even though it smashes all the way across the room from me, I flinch at the sound.

"Just go," he growls in a low voice, turning away, and I start to do just that—but then I stop.

There's something about the way he spoke, the broken and wretched look in his eyes. Like he was filled with self-loathing and despair.

"You know what? No," I vow, stalking closer. "Telling yourself you're just a monster is just taking the easy way out."

He stares at me incredulously for a moment. "What are you talking about?"

"Monsters aren't born, Sebastian. They're made," I tell him, determined. "By the choices you make every day. And you can choose to do better. I've seen that you're capable of it, in the way you take care of your sister, and everything Bianca said, about your charity work and all the good it does," I exclaim. "But you prefer to just go ahead and declare you're irredeemable, because it lifts you off the hook of ever having to try, and fail, and fight to be better like everybody else!"

Sebastian shakes his head, still furious. "You don't know what you're talking about. You don't know the truth about me—"

"I know plenty," I interrupt him, with a sharp laugh. "Believe me, I still have the scars to show for it. So the fact I'm telling you this should mean something. You know, it would be easier for me, too, if you really were rotten to the core," I add bitterly, "But you're not. There's a part of you that wants to be better, even if you can't admit it to yourself!"

Sebastian stares at me. "You don't really believe that..."

"I do," I vow.

"But why?" his voice is edged with desperation now, and he looks so unlike himself, so lost and full of anguish that my heart aches to hold him. To make it better.

"I don't know," I whisper, conflicted. Even as I say the words, I'm fighting it. He's supposed to be my enemy, but here I am, desperately wishing he could become a better man. "I can't explain it, I wish I could. But I do."

We stay there a moment, our gazes locked. The air crackles between us, and then I'm reaching for him, pulling his face down to me in a tormented, fevered kiss.

Sebastian doesn't argue anymore. He just kisses me back like he's a dying man, with nothing to lose.

And I feel the same way: Yanking him closer, greedy for the taste of him, our bodies slamming together against the wall as we stumble back. The heat is all-consuming, the fire of lust between us blazing out of control.

I'm pulling Sebastian's shirt open, as he tears my robe open, and hikes up my nightgown, lifting me up and setting me on his desk. He bends his head, kissing down my neck and palming my breasts as I moan, arching into his hands.

I want him, now.

I *need* him.

Fumbling with his belt, I unzip his pants and free his cock. It springs, hot and hard in my hands. Sebastian sounds a groan, thrusting against me, as I part my legs wider and position him at my core.

He slams inside me, and fuck, it feels like he's coming home.

"Goddamn," Sebastian's voice is raw, and I claw blindly at his shoulders, sobbing out loud as he stretches me open. "How does it feel so good?"

I don't know. Fuck, I don't know anything right now except the weight of his body, and the low groans sounding in the air, and thick invasion as he pistons his hips, working his cock deeper, making my whole body shake with the force of his impact.

"Sebastian..." I sob, clutching hold of him. "Oh God, right there!" I thrust back, eager to take every stroke. The desk creaks as it takes on the weight of our bodies, and my hips are going to be bruised tomorrow from his iron grip, but I don't care. The feel of him is too good. Too deep. He's filling me to the hilt, and it makes all the stress and confusion of the day disappear.

This is all that matters. The two of us, right now.

The pressure starts to build quickly, and we're both panting, clutching hold of each other as if for dear life.

"I want to be better," Sebastian's fevered whisper is almost lost under the sound of our bodies slamming together, but he grips me tightly, his cock embedded deep inside. "For you," he vows, ragged. "I want to be the man you deserve."

"So do it," I gasp mindlessly as my core clenches around him. "Be that man. Be *mine*."

I shatter with a cry, the pleasure taking over the both of us, like we're sharing the same climax, coming undone as a single body.

I hold him, shaken by what just happened—and the emotions tangled in my chest.

I never thought I believed in redemption, and definitely not for a man like Sebastian. I swore I could never forgive him for what he did to Miles, no matter if he ever tried to earn it.

So, what the hell am I saying to him now?

Do I want Sebastian to be a better man for the sake of the world...?

Or simply to justify the way I feel about him, the passion between us that I can never deny?

Chapter 16

Avery

This time, I wake up with Sebastian in bed beside me. I know he's there the second I open my eyes and feel his arm around me, holding me close.

I stretch, yawning. Last night comes rushing back to me: the terrible fight, and all of Sebastian's self-loathing and agony. The sex, somehow more intense than ever.

Our connection...

When I roll to face him, Sebastian is awake, and watching me.

"Good morning," I whisper, watching his face for signs of his mood.

Which Sebastian will I find with me today: the detached, controlled man, or the one who held me all night in his arms?

"Good morning," he echoes, giving me a gentle kiss. I relax into him, full of relief—even edged with self-loathing. "You slept OK?"

"Aside from your snoring," I tease.

He snorts with surprised laughter. "I don't snore."

"Sure you do," I lie, sitting up in bed. "Like a honking great subway train. Could have woken the neighbors."

"Funny how nobody's ever told me about that before." Sebastian smirks.

"Well, you're just lucky I'm here to speak truth to power and tell it like it is," I smile back at him, feeling a warmth in my chest at our careless banter.

"You know, if we're being honest, then I should probably say something about your sleepwalking," Sebastian continues, yawning.

"My what?" I blink in surprise.

"It's more like sleep-karate," he corrects himself. "Flailing and lashing all night, you nearly had my eye out."

"I'm so sorry!" I blurt, mortified—until I see the glint of humor in his eyes. "Hey!" I protest, laughing. I grab a pillow and hit his bare chest. "That's not fair!"

"Turnabout's fair play," he says with a wink. Then he leans up and kisses me again—properly this time, slow, like he's savoring every moment.

I sink against him, tasting him, before finally coming up for air. Sebastian sprawls lazily beside me, reaching to check his phone, one hand resting on my leg.

It really feels like something's changed between us. This is the Sebastian I saw in Italy, but we're not on vacation anymore. I want to say something, ask about the shift, but I don't want to jinx it.

Besides, even I don't know how I feel about this yet. It was true what I yelled at him last night: It was easier when he was just a heartless monster, easy to hate. The shame and self-loathing I've felt because of my desire for him was simple compared to this new treacherous feeling blooming in my chest.

Affection.

"I need coffee," I blurt, not wanting to think about it.

"Your wish is my command." Sebastian gives another yawn and gets out of bed. Uncaring about his nudity, he stretches his arms over his head, and I can't resist watching the way his back muscles tighten and release. He grabs a robe, and some sweatpants, somehow just as attractive in clothes as out of them. "Breakfast in bed?" he offers, with a wolfish smile. "Not that I need to go anywhere to enjoy a feast..."

I blush. "I'll, umm, see you down there," I blurt, feeling like a mess. I gather the duvet around my body and use it to shield myself as I leave the room, ignoring the way that Sebastian chuckles.

"I've seen you naked, you know," he calls out to me, and I smile as I make my way down the hallway to my room.

Away from him, I'm able to catch my breath, and try to think clearly. I don't need to make any decisions about Sebastian's redemption right now. Who even knows if this new, improved version of the man will last? He's been running hot and cold on me since the day we met—emphasis on *cold*.

For all I know, this is just another way of lulling me into a false sense of security, before he yet again reveals his icy excuse for a heart.

Still, there's a part of me that doesn't quite believe that. The look in his eyes last night... It revealed something I've never seen from him before. An inner conflict, a battle that's clearly raging inside of him between his demons and better angels.

But which side will be victorious?

I decide to take a quick shower and leave my hair down to air-dry. When I'm fully dressed, I head downstairs to find him in the kitchen, sipping from a steaming mug of coffee while leaning against the counter. He's dressed in a suit now, devastatingly handsome.

"So, what do you have planned today?" He asks, handing me my own mug.

I think about the message Charlie sent me while we were at the lake. I have to deal with that. I have to find out what she discovered.

Even if I'm not sure what I'm going to do about it.

"I'm not sure, maybe do some more research about college," I lie.

"That sounds good. Let me know if you want my help with anything," Sebastian says, right away, and I feel a stab of guilt.

That's new. The whole point of this has been to lie to the man, but it doesn't feel the same anymore.

"I will, thanks." I take a sip of coffee. "And you have work, I'm guessing. Unless you're off to play racquetball in that outfit."

He chuckles. "Yes, I have some important meetings that I can't miss today. But I'd love to have dinner with you later?"

"Sure," I agree quickly. "Just let me know when and where."

"I'll ask my assistant for the best reservation," he says. "She's always up to date with what's new in town."

"Great."

Sebastian plants a chaste kiss on my lips, and the taste of him lingers even after he walks out the door.

"Breakfast, Miss?" Leon asks, materializing in the doorway. I blink, clearing my foggy mind.

"Umm, yes. Toast would be great, thanks."

Leon fixes me a plate—I've learned by now that it's impossible to even make myself a simple meal here, the kitchen is his domain, and he takes it as a personal insult if I so much as open a bag of chips—and I retreat to the sunroom, to think.

As relaxing as our time in Italy was, the real world—and my real mission—is still waiting. I have dozens of unanswered questions, and with Sebastian's uncle, Richard, lurking in the shadows with his surveillance and agenda, I can't forget that I'm exposed here.

I may be running out of time.

Pulling up Charlie's text message, I make sure Leon isn't around and call the number she included to "book an appointment."

"Stonebridge Spa," Charlie's voice says when she picks up on the first ring. She sounds believable with her serene tone.

"It's Avery Carmicheal," I say brightly, playing along with the act. "Calling to make that appointment we discussed."

"Good to hear from you," she says, "I've been wondering when you'd call."

"My schedule has been busy." I say blandly.

"Well, I've managed to locate the therapist you requested, Terry Hardcastle," Charlie continues.

"Oh."

I should be happy about this. Finding the police officer who was first on the scene of the accident could be a big lead. But now, I have a small knot of dread forming in the base of my stomach.

What if I don't want to know the answers?

"I'll send you the address," Charlie continues. "I would suggest you don't delay in seeing him."

"Thanks," I reply, still conflicted.

We hang up, and the text comes through moments later, with this policeman's current address. I wish I could just ignore it, but I can't, not when I've come this far.

I have to find out if Sebastian is hiding something.

. . .

157

I finish breakfast, and then set out on my journey. I walk on foot a few blocks from Sebastian's house, and then catch a taxi from there to Victoria Station. Terry Hardcastle lives in Wimbledon, an area I only know from the tennis tournament, but it's easy enough to take a train, and then walk when I reach my destination.

When I finally arrive, I find that I'm in a leafy residential area. The home is a modest cottage with a meticulously maintained garden, and I slowly walk up the path and knock on the blue-painted door, that sinking feeling in my stomach back again.

Everything here looks friendly and innocent, but I'm about to go digging up the ghosts of the past.

Ghosts that have stayed buried for the past sixteen years.

There's no answer at the door. I pause. After coming all this way, I can't just leave empty-handed. I see a car in the gravel driveway, so it looks like somebody's home. I follow the garden path around to the back of the cottage. When I round the corner, I see that the beautiful garden continues back here, and there's a man on his knees in a vegetable path, pulling weeds. He's in his fifties, with a weathered face, wearing scruffy corduroy pants and a cable knit sweater.

"Hi there," I call, not wanting to startle him.

He looks up, surprised. "Hello." He gets to his feet, brushing dirt from his knees. "Something I can help you with?"

"Are you Terry Hardcastle?" I ask, hopefully.

"Yeah, that's me. And you are?"

"My name is Avery," I say, pleased I've found the right guy. "And, well, this may seem strange, but I wanted to ask you a couple of questions about an old case of yours."

Terry gives me an assessing look, and I can see that despite his retirement, he's still sharp. "An old case, eh? Are you some kind of reporter?"

"No, nothing like that," I reply quickly. "I'm just... curious."

"Well, I worked on a lot of cases over the years," he says, strolling closer. "What makes you think I'll remember this one?"

I pause. "Do you remember the car accident that killed Patrick Wolfe?"

I can see from the look on his face that he does. But there's more than just familiarity there. I see a flicker of something dark in his eyes.

Is it fear?

Terry clears his throat, gruff. "I don't have anything to say about that."

He turns away from me, back to the garden, but I move closer. "Please, it's important. I read your report," I add quickly. "I know there must be more to what happened."

Terry pauses. "If you've read the report, then you know the facts," he says carefully.

"No, it doesn't add up," I insist. "There's something you wouldn't say. An accident like this, there should have been more attention paid. The press, media, I don't know. But it looks like a cover-up."

"So maybe you should take a hint, and leave the past where it belongs," Terry says firmly. "Believe me, kid, those are powerful people."

"I know." I move to stand directly in front of him, blocking his path. "I'm already tangled up with the Wolfes. I *need* to know the truth. Please," I add, and maybe there's something in my eyes that Terry recognizes, because he exhales.

"I don't have any truths. Just... suspicions."

"I'll take them," I say eagerly. "Whatever you have to say about that night, I want to hear it."

Terry looks at me for a long moment. "Then you better come in and have a cup of tea."

He leads me to the house, and through the back door into the kitchen. He peels off his muddy shoes, and washes up at the farmhouse sink, while I look around. The house is warm and homey, and I see photos of Terry with a wife and adult children, pinned to the refrigerator, and framed on the walls.

"When I arrived at the scene of the accident, there were two cars there," he begins. "One of them, the one with Patrick Wolfe's body inside, was mangled and on fire. I could see Patrick's body inside, and he was already dead. His little girl, Scarlett, was hurt, burned pretty bad." He shakes his head at the memory, putting the tea kettle on the stove. "Some passersby were already tending to her, they'd seen the crash and pulled over."

"What about the other car?" I ask, taking a seat at the table.

"It had been hit head-on," Terry replies. "Looked like the driver had been killed instantly. There were skid marks all over the road, I guess they'd all tried to avoid the collision."

Bianca's father. I wince.

"So... It *was* just a tragic accident?" I ask, frowning.

He pauses. "It looked that way..." he begins, but I can tell, he's not convinced.

"Tell me," I encourage him. "You saw something, didn't you? Something you didn't put in the report. Please, anything could help me. Any details at all."

Terry sighs. "It wasn't right," he says finally, sitting with me at the table. "The accident, it didn't look right. Patrick Wolfe's body was in the passenger seat when I saw it, not behind the wheel. It's possible that he was thrown around in the accident, but... The driver's side door was open. Why didn't he fall, or crawl out that side? And then there was the kid, Scarlett. The people who stopped to help say they found her about twenty yards from the vehicle. She was unconscious. So, how did she get out of the car?"

"She could have crawled, before she passed out?" I offer, but even I know, it doesn't sound right.

Terry nods. "Could have. But she was in a bad way, I just don't see it."

I try to picture the scene in my mind, the crushed front end of the car. The fire. Scarlett hurt and Patrick dead. But all the details Terry just provided allow me to put the pieces together.

"You think someone else was there?" I ask, feeling a chill.

He nods, reluctant. "I think someone else was driving. Someone else caused the crash."

My heart stops.

"Are you sure?" I whisper. Whatever I was expecting to hear from him, it wasn't this.

Terry gives a wry chuckle. "I'm not sure of anything, but I suspect that the person behind the wheel, the one responsible for the accident, pulled Scarlett out and then fled the scene before anyone arrived. Leaving those two bodies behind."

I gulp. "Do you have a suspect?" I venture.

But I don't really have to ask. I already know what he's about to say.

"The son." Terry gives a grim nod. "Sebastian Wolfe."

Sebastian.

I feel a chill, just hearing his name.

I'm a monster.

That's what he told me, his voice full of guilt and despair. But I never could have imagined this is what he meant.

"If that's what you thought, why didn't you put it in your report?" I ask, still reeling.

Terry snorts. "Oh, I tried, alright. But my superiors shut down my questions and made me alter my report. The remains of Patrick Wolfe's car were shipped off before they could be properly analyzed," he explains, even as I'm having trouble focusing. Sebastian wouldn't have done this. Could he? "The forensics guy suddenly took a fancy new job at a private company that was linked to Wolfe Capital," Terry continues. "It all paints quite a picture, don't you think?"

"D-did you question him? Sebastian, I mean?" My voice is weak, and I almost feel dazed. "Was there any real proof linking him to the accident?"

Terry sighs. "I asked around as best I could, but my bosses wanted to sweep the whole thing under the rug. Rumor has it that Sebastian and his dad had been fighting in the days leading up to the accident. And that boy was already known for having a hair-trigger temper." He scowls. "I went to see him, right after the accident. To break the news to his mum. The guy had no alibi during the time of the accident, and he was sporting a fresh bruise on his forehead. Said it was a sports injury, but I didn't buy it. After that, he lawyered up fast. I couldn't get near him. The bosses made it clear, no more questions. Sign the report and move on. I didn't have much of a choice."

"Could it have been someone else in the car?" I ask, almost desperately. Would Sebastian have caused that crash, and then just left his father's body?

Was Patrick even dead yet?

"Anything is possible, I guess. But I'll you one thing." Terry's expression turns grave, and I felt a chill run down my spine. "I've interviewed killers before, and I know the look they have in their eyes. The control. The anger. The detached cold-ness. I saw it in Sebastian Wolfe, and I won't forget it, I'm telling you that."

I swallow hard around the lump in my throat. "And you never said anything to anyone before now?"

"Like who? Who's going to go up against a family with that kind of influence? But I've watched him over the years, rising to power and wealth." Terry scowls. "It's disgusting that he can just walk away from what happened and live the high life. It's not right. There should be consequences. The man's got blood on his hands."

I lurch to my feet, feeling sick to my stomach.

Blood on his hands... I thought that before, with Miles, but now...

Now I can't believe Sebastian is capable of doing such damage—and just walking away.

"Thank you for your time," I tell him hurriedly. "I won't keep you anymore."

Terry gets up, too, and shows me to the door. "Listen, kid, I don't know how you're mixed up with these people, but I suggest you put distance between yourself and that family, especially Sebastian. He's dangerous."

I leave, still reeling. I replay the night that we stayed with his mom and Richard at their country house. That was when he told me about the accident that killed his father. The trauma he felt from it was obvious, and I assumed it all about losing a loved one. I could relate to that, after all.

But how much of that was grief... and how much was *guilt?*

Is this what makes him think he's a monster? Even if it was just a tragic accident, surely, he wouldn't feel this way.

Unless it wasn't. Unless Terry is right, and Sebastian somehow wanted to harm his father. I don't want to believe it, but haven't I seen glimpses of his cold fury myself?

If it was a fight, if things got out of hand...

Did Sebastian leave his father to die?

I don't know, but either way, I can't ignore it.

I have to learn the truth.

Chapter 17

Avery

I don't go straight back to Sebastian's house. Instead, I find myself in the library again. I didn't plan it, but I feel lost and all I can think to do is gather more information. I end up combing through the archives from the year of the accident, even though I've been through them before. It's not exactly a surprise when I don't find anything new, but I can't help feeling disappointed.

I guess I'm trying to find something that will convince me Terry's wrong.

I don't want to believe this.

The only way I'll know for sure is if I ask Sebastian.

When I arrive back at the house, I hear music coming from the kitchen. It's classic rock, and I follow the sound to find Sebastian there, cooking dinner. I blink in surprise. He's chopping vegetables, looking relaxed with his sleeves rolled up and collar open.

When he see me, he smiles. "I was just about to call you. Dinner will be ready soon."

"Dinner?" I glance around to see if the staff is here, but

Sebastian turns to the stove and shakes a sauté pan. *"You're cooking?"* I check again.

He chuckles. "No need to sound so surprised. I am a capable man."

"I know," I answer automatically, conflict still churning in my chest. I take a seat on the barstool at the kitchen island and watch him move effortlessly around the kitchen. "You're in a good mood," I note quietly.

He smiles. "It was a good day at work. At least, there were no problems. In my business, any day without a catastrophe is a successful one."

I pause. "That sounds exhausting."

"It is, but I like it." He shrugs. "I've always been the type to thrive when I'm challenged." Sebastian adds the vegetables to the pan. "Now, how about some wine? I have a dry red in the wine cellar that you'll love."

I manage a smile. "That sounds great."

He leaves the room, and I pause, torn. But I don't have much time. If I'm going to do this...

Don't be weak now, Avery.

I quickly pull out my phone and set it to record. Then I position it under a magazine in the middle of the counter. Anything Sebastian says will be perfectly captured.

My heart is pounding when Sebastian returns with the wine. "Do I want to know how old this is?" I quip nervously, as he opens it and pours.

"Older than the both of us," he replies with a smile. "Cheers."

"Cheers," I echo, clinking my glass to his and taking a tiny sip.

He turns back to the food, and I wonder how I'm going to ask him about the accident.

"So, what did you do today?" he asks, glancing over at me.

"Did you decide anything more about college? I told you, I have a lot of contacts, so if there's a program you'd like, just say the word. I can have everything arranged."

I nod slowly. "Actually... I wasn't looking into that today. I was talking to a man named Terry Hardcastle."

Sebastian's back is turned to me, but I see him freeze at the mention of the name. He stops moving for a long moment, and I start to wonder if he's even going to respond. Then, he very deliberately turns to face me.

"What are you playing at?" his voice is low.

I swallow hard. I'm in dangerous territory here. "I'm not playing," I say, hoping that my voice doesn't give away how nervous I feel. "This isn't a game."

"You think I don't know that?" Sebastian demands. "Fuck, Avery... What the hell are you doing digging up the past?"

"Because I need to know what happened to you!" I exclaim. "Sebastian, all these secrets... You can't go on like this. Just tell me the truth!"

"It's none of your goddamn business." Sebastian snarls, fists clenching at his sides.

Dammit.

I can see him shutting down: The walls going up, rendering him unreadable and distant. After everything... I know I have to try and get through to him. Before it's too late.

"Was it you?" I blurt, my voice ringing out in the silence of the kitchen. "Were you driving the car, that night? When your father died?"

There's a beat of silence, and I wonder if I've gone too far.

Then Sebastian exhales, and all the fight seems to go out of him.

He nods. "Yes."

It's just one word, but the sound is so broken, I gasp. "Sebastian..."

He meets my eyes in a look of such bottomless guilt and regret, he's almost unrecognizable. "It was me," he continues, sounding hollow. "I was driving that night. And it's haunted me every day of my life since then."

We stand there, frozen, on either side of the kitchen island. My mind is racing, and my heart?

My heart aches for the dejection in his gaze. Because that's not the look of a cold-blooded killer. It's the expression of a lost, guilty man, haunted by his past.

A past he can never repair.

Instinct drives me to close the space between us. I take his hands, staring urgently into his eyes. "Talk to me, Sebastian. You don't have to hide it anymore. Tell me what happened."

He takes a ragged breath. I can see the war play out behind his eyes, and I don't know what makes him decide, but finally, he speaks.

"I was with them that night." His voice is low. Aching. "I'd just gotten my learner's permit, and I wanted to drive. Dad said 'No'. It was dark out, and the roads were wet, but I insisted. I was so sure I could handle everything, but a deer ran out in the road, and I tried to swerve and... I lost control."

He swallows hard, and I can see the memories in his eyes. "I can still hear Scarlett screaming from the backseat. I tried to brake," he adds, haunted. "But I couldn't get the car back under control. And then there were headlights, another vehicle heading straight for us..."

Sebastian pauses, looking down. "It was chaos. I hit my head on the steering wheel, I was pretty disoriented, and when I came around... Dad was already gone. At least, I thought he was."

I squeeze his hands. "I'm so sorry."

"The car was on fire," Sebastian continues. "I didn't know what to do. Scarlett was unconscious, and bleeding. I smashed a window and dragged her out. And then... I went for help," he says, looking me in the eye again. "I know nobody believes me, but I went to get help. But... It was too late. I thought my dad was dead, and that other man... I panicked. I didn't know what to do."

"So you didn't go back." I finish for him, understanding the whole story now. "You pretended like you'd never been there at all."

Sebastian nods. "They said it was just an accident, and it was. But not the way they thought it happened."

"But if it was a deer, and you lost control, why didn't you say something?" I ask, frowning. "Nobody could have blamed you."

"I was scared. I was still young, and people were dead. I killed them, whether it was an accident or not," Sebastian repeats, full of anguish and self-loathing. "And then, afterward, all I could think was... What if I could have saved them? My dad, and Bianca's father? What if I could have done something, anything... But instead, I ran. I was a coward," he says bitterly. "My mother was devastated, and Richard... He swept in with the lawyers and told me to keep my mouth shut."

"So he knows?" my eyes widen.

Sebastian nods. "We've never said it out loud, but... Yeah. He made the whole thing go away, somehow. Payoffs, I'm guessing. He said that my mother needed me now, that we had to protect everything my father had built. We just needed to move on and put the whole thing behind us."

Sebastian pauses. "Sometimes, I think it would have been better, if I'd come clean. Even if they'd prosecuted me for manslaughter, or reckless driving, I don't know... Prison couldn't have been worse than living with this secret."

I have no words, so I just keep a hold of his hand and listen.

"You know, I always wondered why Richard protected me,"

Sebastian adds, a note of bitterness in his voice. "Maybe it's to keep his power over me. He could try to destroy me with this, any time he likes."

"Maybe he's worried he'd be implicated because of the bribes," I offer. "Or maybe he really does want to spare your family any more grief."

Sebastian gives a nod. Then he seems to realize I'm still holding him.

He pulls away. "It doesn't matter," he says abruptly. "Now you know the truth. You know what I'm capable of, the damage I've caused in my life. You're better off without me."

My heart breaks for him.

He's been so alone in this. Weighed down by his grief, and the guilt that he could have done more to stop it.

I know how that kind of guilt can eat away at you. Haven't I felt it myself, deep down, wondering if I could have kept Miles from taking his own life?

"It wasn't your fault," I insist. "It was an accident. A terrible accident. You didn't mean to hurt anyone. You protected Scarlett. You *saved* her."

Sebastian shakes his head. "It doesn't matter. Not enough."

"Yes, it does," I insist. "You're making a difference in the world, even if you don't realize it. Look at your foundation. How many people have you helped?"

"It's not enough." Sebastian shakes his head. "It doesn't come close to erasing what I did."

"But you can make amends," I urge him. "You can do your father proud, if you choose to. If you make the choice to try. You're not a lost cause," I insist, not even realizing I believe it until the words are out of my mouth. "Nobody is, if they truly want to change."

Sebastian looks at me. "Where did you come from?" he

asks, with a note of wonder in his voice. He pulls me into his arms, holding me tightly. "Were you sent here to save me?"

No, I came to destroy you.

The guilt is heavy on my heart. He wouldn't say any of this if he knew my cellphone was still buried under those magazines on the countertop, recording every word. But I don't get a chance to dwell on it as Sebastian presses a kiss to my lips.

It's deep and desperate, as he molds his lips to mine, his free hand going to my waist and pulling me closer until my body is flush against his. The kiss ignites something in me, the same desperate wish to block out the past, and only focus on the two of us, right here.

Sebastian draws back. "You're still here," he says, looking down at me.

"Of course I am," I reply, confused.

"I always thought, if anyone knew... They'd leave me," he explains. "I never got close to anyone, because I knew, this day would come. They'd learn the truth... And they'd be gone."

I pull him closer. "I'm not going anywhere," I vow, ignoring my confusion, and all the questions now brimming over in my mind.

"I can't believe it, after all this time." Sebastian looks at me with wonder and clear relief. "I won't keep any more secrets between us. I swear it." he pauses. "I love you, Avery."

My head snaps up. "What?" I stare at him in disbelief.

Sebastian takes my hands. "I said I love you," he repeats it, searching my eyes. "In fact... Marry me."

What?

Am I hallucinating? I gape at him. After everything that's happened between us, the secrets I've dug up, and the revenge I've been planning, there's no way Sebastian Wolfe just proposed to me.

But he did.

Sebastian seems amused by my shock. He chuckles. "I know, it's sudden, but... I mean it. There's something between us, it's more powerful than anything I've ever felt before. We can't deny it, and God knows we've tried," he adds, wry.

"But..." my head spins.

"I know you'll need to think about it, but I know what I want," he tells me, totally in control again. Determined. *Fearsome.* "It's you. Only you. Marry me, Avery. Be my wife, and we can start over. We'll make a new future together and leave the past behind."

I stand there, totally stunned. My mind racing to find a way to tell him 'No'...

... And deny the small part of my heart that wants to say 'Yes'.

Chapter 18

Avery

Sebastian wants me to marry him.

I'm in a daze the next day, still trying to wrap my head around his shocking proposal. It's hard to believe. After everything we've been through, all the cruel moves he's made—and my own deceitful plotting—even considering it is out of the question. I'd have to be out of my mind to think about pledging to be his wife and embarking on this fresh start he seems determined to bring about.

It's out of the question. But still...

My heart aches for him. He was right: There's something between us, beyond logic or reason. An inexplicable connection that's drawn me back to him a dozen times, already. And now that I finally know the secret he's been hiding, and all the ways we're more alike than I ever imagined, I can't help feel that connection calling inside me.

Wanting to be with him.

Wanting to believe that despite the odds, we could actually be happy together.

But what does that make me?

A traitor, to Miles' memory, and everything I've sworn to avenge. My feelings for Sebastian go against everything I ever believed in, the whole reason I came into his life in the first place. *To destroy it.*

But looking back now on the raging girl who made that vow, I almost don't recognize myself. I've changed.

Sebastian has changed me.

I don't know what to say to him about the proposal, but he seems to understand I need time to think it through. He leaves for work, somehow seeming lighter and unburdened since his dark confession, and I'm left alone to mull the future.

Because he isn't the only one who has choices to make about who he is and what he wants to do with his life. The same questions apply to me, too, and I don't even know where to begin. I have the recording of him confessing that he was driving the car that night. It could be the evidence I've been waiting for to destroy him...

If I choose to use it.

I'm lost in my thoughts, when my phone buzzes with a text. It's Charlie, using the same spa code.

'*Your appointment is confirmed: Today, 1pm.*' There's an address, too, so it must be something important. Glad for the distraction, I get dressed and cross the city, to what turns out to be a chic, elegant hotel just off Regent Street.

I enter through the gleaming lobby, looking around for Charlie's familiar face.

But instead, I see a ghost. At least, that's how it feels when I lay eyes on him.

Nero.

"Avery!" Lily's voice comes, enthusiastic, and then she's rushing across the lobby and pulling me into a hug, smothering me in blonde hair and a silk scarf. "Oh my God, I've missed you!"

I hug her back, suddenly overwhelmed by this visit from my former life. "I've missed you, too." I tell her in a daze, pulling away as Nero saunters over to meet us, looking smart, but still every inch the dangerous mob boss.

"What part of 'discreet' don't you understand?" he chides Lily, good-naturedly. "We're supposed to be keeping a low profile."

"Sorry," she grins. "I was just so happy to see Avery again. Avery?" She pauses, noticing my emotion. And maybe it's the stress of my choice that I'm facing, or suddenly seeing old friends like this, but I do the unthinkable. Something I never would have imagined in a million years.

I burst into tears, and cry.

"Well, you sure know how to make an entrance."

An hour later, and I'm cloistered away in a booth in the hotel restaurant with Lily, indulging in tea and cake and all the girl talk I can handle. Nero has made himself scarce, probably sensing that we need a chance to catch up on things—and that his brutal style of conflict-resolution might not be what I need right now.

"I'm sorry," I apologize again, self-conscious about my tears. "It's just... so much has happened. I've been keeping it together on my own here for so long, it felt like two entirely different lives were colliding when I saw you walk in."

"There's no need to apologize," Lily reassures me, her face open and friendly. "Hell, I know a thing or two about worlds colliding. And annoyingly handsome men keeping me locked up as a prisoner," she quips with a knowing grin.

I have to laugh. Things weren't easy between her and Nero when they got together. He was pretty much forcing her to pose as his fiancée under the threat of death, as revenge for her father informing on the Barrettis when they were younger. They say there's a fine line between love and hate, and those two definitely proved that to be true.

Still, I feel a rush of shame as I fill her in on everything that's happened between Sebastian and me since I first arrived, vowing my revenge.

"I don't know how, but the lines just got more blurred," I despair, drowning my sorrows in English tea. "It's not just desire, either. Although the sexual connection is just..."

"Mind-blowing? Earth-shaking?" Lily suggests. "Epic despite the fact you want to throttle him and also beg for more in the same breath? Been there. Done that."

I manage a smile. At least someone knows what it's like to want someone and loathe them equally fiercely. "All that, and more," I admit. "But now... my emotions are involved, too. I can't believe it, but I've fallen for him. What the hell is wrong with me?" I despair. "This was never the plan!"

"But plans change," Lily says sympathetically. "I mean, look at me and Nero. I wanted him dead, and now, well, I still want to kill him sometimes, but only in a good way." She lifts her teacup, and I see the enormous diamond flashing on her ring finger. Proof that she and Nero found a way through all their animosity and doubts.

"But... How did you know Nero was worth forgiving after everything he did?" I ask. "How could you trust that he really wanted to change?"

Lily sighs and sets her tea down. She doesn't speak for a long moment, and I'm on the edge of my seat, waiting for her to get her thoughts together.

"It's faith," she answers finally. "Belief in things yet unseen. In the end, Nero *earned* my forgiveness for all the shit he put me through, but even before that... *Way* before that, actually... My heart was his. I couldn't change it or deny it." She gives a small shrug. "The damn thing has a mind of its own, apparently, and it wouldn't have it any other way."

"That sounds familiar," I say with a sigh. "It's like I have a million reasons not to trust him, or want to be with him, but the only thing that matters is... I want him. Not just his body, but all of him. But how can I feel that way, when he's hurt so many people?"

"I've asked myself that question a few times, too," Lily agrees. "Nero is no saint. But he's put the mafia world behind him now. He's gone legit—to keep me safe. That counts for something."

I nod slowly. Nobody expected the ruthless Nero Barretti to turn his life upside down for love, but he's done it. He would burn the whole world to the ground, if Lily said she'd like the ashes as a prize.

"Would Sebastian make the same sacrifice for me?" I wonder. "He's a man who's spent his life chasing more: more money, more status, more power... Where do I fit into that? Am I another shiny acquisition to him? Or did he mean it when he said he wanted us to build a new future together?"

"Only you can answer that question," Lily says with regret. "And it's not just about his choices, either. This is about you, too," her voice turns into a warning. "You have to be willing to be honest with him. Truly forgive him for everything he's done. Sebastian... He's not Nero," she adds, gravely. "I don't know if he's worth it."

Her words linger with me, even after I say my goodbyes to her and Nero, and leave the hotel. I walk, not paying attention to the tourists and shoppers around me. I'm still lost in thought about the choice I face.

Because Lily was right: This isn't just about what Sebastian chooses to do with his future, but about me, and whether I can find it in my heart to truly forgive him for everything he's done. Because I know that if I can't, if I cling to my resentment and bitterness over Miles, then I'll just be creating a prison for myself in this relationship. I'll never escape the past, no matter what else we do.

Do I have that kind of forgiveness in me?

I don't know. I walk for hours, but I'm no closer to an answer, so I look around to get my bearings, and figure out hailing a cab for home.

I'm beside a newsstand, and my eyes land on a headline, as the owner sets out the afternoon edition.

'Shipping shock – Dunleavey dead.'

I freeze. "Can I see that?" I blurt, grabbing for a paper.

The man scowls. "Seventy pence," he insists, and I fumble in my wallet for change before he finally hands one over.

I flip the page, searching out the story. There.

'Shipping tycoon Alistair Dunleavey was found dead at his home in Essex, after an apparent overdose. Police are investigating whether the death was intentional, as Dunleavey had been reported to have been acting erratically after the hostile takeover of his family firm by Wolfe Capital...'

My stomach lurches, and I'm in danger of losing the tea and cake I just consumed. I feel a cold chill wash over me as I slowly lower the newspaper.

Suicide?

I can't believe it. Then I remember, Lulu works for this newspaper. I quickly write a text to her.

'Just saw the news about Alistair Dunleavy. Is it true?'

Her reply comes quickly and it's short.

Yes, very tragic. He left a note. His wife found him, poor woman.

My knees start to buckle, and I steady myself on a nearby

railing. The world is spinning, and in my mind, I'm no longer standing on a street corner in London.

It all comes back in a sickening rush. Just a few months ago, and an ocean away, but it feels like yesterday...

"Miles?" I call, pounding on his door. "Come on, we'll be late. The movie starts at seven."

There's no reply, but when I try the handle, it swings open. Unlocked.

"Miles?" I call again, immediately on my guard. I haven't heard from Miles all day, but I figured, he was just busy dealing with Nero's latest legal wrangling.

I reach for the flick knife I keep in my boots, taking a step into the hallway. Even though things have been quiet for the Barrettis after Nero brokered a truce, I'm always alert for danger.

And this feels wrong.

"You're the one who wanted to see this thing," I call, keeping my voice light, even as I prowl, knife raised, towards the living room. "I would be happy just grabbing a beer and a bite."

I look around. Nothing looks out of place. Miles is a neat freak, and prides himself on a well kept living space, so I would notice if there was a sign of a struggle, or anything out of place. I continue on, searching the kitchen, and then moving on down the hall towards his office.

The words die on my lips as I take in the sight of him, hanging from the rafter.

I scream, rushing to him. Trying to lift his body, trying to get him down. In the end, I remember the knife in my hand, and manage to drag a chair over, and saw, jagged, through the length of rope he has strung around the beam.

"Miles! Open your eyes, oh God, please."

But he doesn't. Not when I loosen the rope that's almost embedded in his neck, or shake his limp body furiously, or even press my mouth to his, trying desperately to resuscitate him.

He doesn't move or make a sound.

He stays dead.

"Dear, are you alright?"

The voice of an older woman pulls me out of the past, but I'm disoriented as I look around. The flashback is so clear in my mind, I could swear, I was right back in that room, shaking with grief.

"You look like you're going to be sick."

My eyes finally land on the woman speaking. She's holding onto a stroller with one hand and holding her phone in the other. She looks so concerned.

"Can I call someone for you? Do you need a lift somewhere? Or an ambulance?"

"No," I manage to say. "I'm fine." My voice is a harsh croak, and I can see that it just worried the woman more, but I don't have a drop of energy to spare reassuring her.

Besides, I'm *not* okay.

I start to walk again, moving on autopilot this time. All the memories I've been holding back are taking over now. Waiting with the body for the cops and Barretti guys. Calling Miles' family. And the funeral... God, that bleak, depressing day as we all stood by the graveyard, watching his coffin disappear into the earth.

Ashes to ashes, dust to dust.

Even now, I can recite Miles' suicide note from memory, it's burned that deeply into my mind.

· · ·

I fucked up. I got in too deep with Sebastian's card game, I tried covering from the accounts, I thought I could win it back again, but I failed. I let you down. I'm sorry.

Sebastian.

The name sends another wave of nausea through me. How could I let myself forget the damage he does? Could a few passionate nights and sweet nothings really wipe clean the legacy of cruelty and pain he's made in this world?

Somehow, I manage to make it home. I'm still in shock, reeling, but I hear voices coming from Sebastian's office. A number of people, all of them sounding worried and urgent.

I drift closer to the open door. Listening, unseen, as they argue inside.

"We need a unified strategy," one woman is saying. "Should we draft a press release?"

"No release," Sebastian says bluntly. "Wolfe Capital has no comment."

"I have to agree with Sukie," a voice from the speakerphone pitches in. "The negative PR from Dunleavey's death will be a hit. He was well-liked and respected in the industry. We don't want to be left playing defense."

"Can we put it around that this was nothing to do with the takeover?" someone else suggests.

"I like that," Sukie nods. "Plant some stories that he was using drugs, or acting erratically, long before the merger talks started. Maybe that was even the reason the board was so eager to accept our offer, they'd already lost faith in his leadership."

I watch, aghast, as they casually discuss smearing a good man's reputation, just to save themselves some bad publicity.

Surely Sebastian can't go along with this?

But he listens calmly to all their proposals, then nods. "I'd rather not get involved for now, I think it's a non-story that will blow over quickly, but just in case, let's prep for Sukie's PR offensive. I'll assess the media attention in the coming days, and we can be ready to deploy if things move against us. What matters is that Wolfe Capital will be posting record profits if we follow the restructuring plan."

I listen to him in horror. What really matters is his profits right now?

"And will you attend the funeral?" someone asks.

Sebastian gives a derisive snort. "I have better things to do than go where I'm not welcome. Moving on: Luke, where are we on the southeast Asian numbers?"

I stumble back from the door. I can't believe it. I feel like the blinders have just fallen from my eyes, and I'm seeing Sebastian for who he truly is again.

The corporate raider. The merciless villain. The man that treats human life so casually—coming behind profits on his priority list.

God, how could I have been such a food? Thinking he wanted to change, that there was a good man hiding beneath all his torment and pain? He can act like he feels bad about the past, but it's just that: an act. He has a trail of bodies littered behind him now. *Patrick Wolfe, Bianca's father, Miles, Alistair Dunleavy....* And while he may not have held a gun to their heads and pulled the trigger, he's killed them in every way that matters.

It's their blood on his hands.

He's destroyed countless lives without thinking twice, and he'll just keep doing it.

Unless somebody stops him.

I pause by the staircase, my resolve hardening into a shard of pure steel. I came here with the task of finding what he loves most and taking it away from him, just like he did to me.

Well, he loves *me* now.

And I know what I have to do.

"Avery?"

I turn. Sebastian has emerged from the office, looking pleased to see me. "I didn't expect to see you back," he says, approaching. "Sorry about the full house," he adds, nodding back to his office. "Just boring business details, nothing important."

Nothing important... I try not to let my disgust show as he drops a casual kiss on my lips.

When he pulls away, I take a deep breath. No point in delaying this.

"I've been thinking about your proposal," I begin. "I have an answer for you."

Sebastian pauses, searching my face. "You do?"

I nod, sick to my stomach—but determined. *This man must pay.*

"Yes, I'll marry you," I tell him, and seal both of our fates. "I want to be your wife."

Chapter 19

Avery

The next week flies past. I told Sebastian that I wanted a big celebration for our engagement party. It's a happy occasion, after all, and will mark a new beginning in our lives together, so, he gave me total freedom to plan whatever I wanted.

What I wanted, was a blowout affair at his estate on Lake Como, with all his business associates and family invited, press, and all to witness our love. And with his unlimited funds, the event planners I hired have pulled it off. The party will take place tonight, at the chateau.

And I can't wait.

"You look beautiful."

Sebastian's voice comes from my bedroom doorway, and I see him in the mirror, looking happy and relaxed. "Thank you, baby," I turn, smoothing down my dress. It's a dark red gown, sweeping to the floor, with a strapless bodice and slim fitted cut. The color of blood.

The color of revenge.

"You're not looking too bad yourself," I add, giving him a

besotted grin. Now that I'm set on my path, the lying has come so much easier. I no longer have doubts or conflict holding me back.

I know exactly what I need to do.

Sebastian comes closer, and I smooth down the lapels of his tuxedo. "I like you in this tux."

"You'll like me more out of it." Sebastian dips his head to kiss my bare shoulder, already sliding his hands over my body. "God, Avery, I've been going crazy wanting you..."

"And you'll just have to wait a little longer," I beam, ducking out of his embrace. I told him I wanted to wait until after the party before having sex again, to make it special. I don't know why, but he bought it, so at least I've been spared the feel of his touch and my own self-loathing for enjoying it. "After the party," I warn him.

He groans. "What if we skip the party, and have a private celebration?"

"Seb!" I protest. "We have people waiting. Lots of people. They all came to share this happy occasion with us and celebrate our future."

I beam some more. I can't believe he's buying my breathless act, but he must truly be in love with me—or half out of his mind with lust—because Sebastian just smiles indulgently.

"You're right. I wouldn't have needed all this show, but this is a good way to kick off our fresh start. Speaking of, I have something for you." He reaches into his pocket and pulls out a little black box. "Every bride-to-be needs an engagement ring."

He opens the box, and even I have to admit that, objectively, it's a stunning ring. Princess-cut, flawless... Simple but a statement.

"It's perfect," I say, as he slides it on my finger. I hold it up to admire the sparkle. I may as well enjoy it while I can. Because this engagement won't last the night. And I'm pretty sure it's not proper etiquette to keep the ring after you've utterly destroyed your fiancé. "Thank you, baby. I love it."

And I'm going to love it even more when I get to throw it in your face.

"I'm glad." He lifts my hand to his lips and kisses my knuckles. I try not to flinch.

"You ready to head downstairs and show it off?" he asks.

I giggle, unwilling to let him suspect anything is coming, even for just a second.

"Let's do it."

I loop my arm through his and he leads us out of the bedroom and down the stairs. I've spent the week with the most famed event planners around who made sure that everything is perfect, and now, I look out at the packed party outside with satisfaction.

There are hundreds of people here, who have flown in from all over the world, and the event spills effortlessly from the terrace to the rolling lawns overlooking the lake. Hundreds of tea lights are strung in a twinkling canopy, and lavish floral decorations of roses and peonies spill from every surface and balustrade, making it look like a fairytale wonderland. A band plays, and people are chatting and mingling, drinking champagne, and there's a buzz of anticipation in the cool night air.

As we approach the party, people rush to congratulate us. "I'm so happy for you," his mother, Trudy, coos.

"Thank you," Sebastian replies, smiling widely.

"Congratulations," Richard adds, with a smarmy grin. "And you too, little missy," he adds, giving me a gross wink. "Taming the bachelor, eh? Well played, indeed."

Eww.

I smile, and play along, picking out familiar faces in the crowd. As well as Sebastian's family, I recognize some top players from Wolfe Capital... Bianca and Violetta, with their friends... plus important people from the London social scene: financiers, entrepreneurs with their model girlfriends, and even a few celebrities, too. It's clearly the ticket of the season. Not a single person is here for me, of course, but that doesn't matter.

They're not guests—they're witnesses, for what's going to happen tonight.

I spot Lulu, over by the stage. "I just need to go powder my nose," I tell Sebastian, and then leave him to field more praise, as I slip away to rendezvous with Lulu.

"This way," I murmur, discreetly leading her inside the house, to a quiet corner just off the living room. When I'm sure we're alone, I drop my voice. "Is it all set?" I ask.

Lulu nods and pulls a draft of the article she's written out of her purse. "I've run everything past my editor and the legal department. The story is going to print tonight, which means it'll be live online in... a few minutes."

I take the draft and skim the article.

'Wolfe Capital's Killer Secrets!" the headline blares.

"Subtle," I remark, pleased.

"Yeah, well, you said you wanted a splash," Lulu replies.

I met with her last week and told her everything I learned about the accident. I even included the cellphone recording I took the night that Sebastian admitted he was driving the car and caused the crash that killed his father. I can see that she quoted it several times in the article.

"It's perfect." I say, lowering the page. "The truth will finally come out."

"Are you sure about this?" Lulu asks, looking at me warily. "A bombshell like this... It's going to make waves. Sebastian's reputation will be ruined, and he might face criminal charges, too."

"Yes, I'm sure."

"But—"

"You wanted a real scoop, didn't you?" I talk over her protest. "Well, here it is. It'll make your career. So maybe just ask fewer questions and be happy with your promotion."

Lulu looks at me, shock and confusion on her face. But then she slowly nods, just like I knew she would. "You don't have long," she says, checking her phone. "The article will go live online at nine, British time. So whatever you're planning now... Make the most of it."

"Oh, I will."

I flash a smile, and then leave her, heading back out to the party. It's in full swing as I return, and Sebastian is just getting onstage with the band, gesturing for silence.

"Speech!" someone in the crowd calls, and everyone laughs, and hushes to listen.

"I want to thank everyone for coming out tonight," Sebastian begins, looking out at the crowd. "First of all, this party was planned by Avery, so let's give her a hand for such a wonderful event."

There's more applause, and I just wave at everyone, trying to look a little shy.

"But you know, she's done more than that," Sebastian continues. "Over the last couple of months, this woman has changed my life. She's opened my eyes to what happiness is, and I love her for that. I never thought I'd find someone to be a true partner in life, but that's what she's become to me."

Someone's phone sounds the *PING* of an alert. Sebastian pauses but keeps talking. "Now, it may seem out of character for me to host a party like this, but it was important to us to share this event—"

Beep. Beep.

All around me, people's phones start going off. A whisper grows, spreading through the room. It turns to a hum, shocked and scandalized, as people read their messages, and look back at the stage with horror in their eyes.

This is it.

Sebastian keeps going for a moment, trying to give his speech in earnest despite the fact that so many people are distracted. Then, one of his PR clambers awkwardly onto the stage, and tugs his sleeve urgently. "What is it?" Sebastian's annoyed demand echoes through the microphone, before she pulls him away, and shows him her cellphone screen.

I can't resist watching his face as he reads the article. It doesn't take him long.

He looks up, slack-jawed. Searching the crowd until he finds me. I can see the confusion in his eyes—and the questions there, as he looks at me.

I raise my glass of champagne glass in his direction, and smile before taking a sip.

Victory tastes sweet.

Realization dawns on his face, followed by disbelief—and a furious rage. He gets down from the stage, charging through the crowd towards me, as everyone watches, riveted.

But before he can reach me, Richard, moves to intercept him.

"I knew this day would come," he says with a smirk. "I can't believe you thought you'd get away with it, but now you're going to get what you deserve." His voice rises, ringing with false indignation. He's grandstanding for the crowd, making it clear he didn't know. "I'm calling an emergency board meeting immediately. I guarantee you'll be removed, and *I'll* take back the company."

Sebastian ignores him, and keeps moving, straight to me. He grabs my arm without a word, and practically drags me back away from the crowd, to a quiet spot on the terrace.

"Why?" he demands. It's a single word, full of pain and anger.

I finally allow my true feelings to show. "Why do you think?" I shoot back at him. "It's because you were right, you're a monster. There's no redeeming someone like you. You'll just keep hurting people, unless someone steps up and stops you."

"Keep hurting who?" Sebastian looks genuinely bewildered.

I give a bitter laugh. "Of course, you don't even realize. There are so many options, you can't even narrow it down. Well, let me help you out with this one. His name was Miles Romano, and you drove him to his death."

Sebastian stares at me, and then barks a laugh of disbelief. "This is because of *him?*"

"He was ten times the man you'll ever be!" I cry, infuriated by his surprise. "But you ruined him, made him think he couldn't keep living. I swore I'd bring him justice, and now I have. You'll finally face the consequences for the choices you've made." I vow, wanting to see Sebastian break too. To beg for mercy or show his fear at what's to come.

But Sebastian just gives a scornful laugh. The look of betrayal is gone, now there's just the icy cruel expression I know too well. "Choices? That's rich. Tell me, Little Sparrow, why is it that you're so quick to blame me for what happened, but not hold Miles accountable for his choices?" He prowls closer, pointing. "It was his choice to join my game, and gamble more than he could afford. His choice to stay at the table, for hand after hand, even when his pot was empty."

I shake my head, tears in my eyes. "No," I protest, not wanting to hear this, but Sebastian doesn't stop.

"It was your beloved Miles' choice to steal from Nero to cover his losses. To keep his failures secret. And, yes, it was all his own choice to take the coward's way out and kill himself instead of facing the consequences of his poor decisions."

Grief and rage erupt inside me. "You bastard!" I sob, swinging out my hand to hit him, but he catches my wrist and holds it in place. "You're a liar! Miles was a good man before he met you! It's all your fault."

"And you're foolish and naïve." Sebastian releases me, looking down with contempt in his eyes. "That picture you've conjured of Miles is a lie. The perfect man you've been carrying this torch for never really existed. And do you want to know what the most pathetic thing is?" he adds, lips curling in a cruel smirk. "The man you've been fighting so long to avenge never loved you at all. If he had, he'd have told you so, even once. Fought to be with you. But he didn't, did he?"

Sebastian taunts me with the aching truth, and the answer must be written all over my stricken face, because he laughs. "I thought so. Miles never reciprocated your hopeless little crush. He never cared at all. Because if he had, I can tell you, he wouldn't have left you like this: broken, desperate, and all alone in the world."

His words cut me to the core.

Oh God. I break down, sobbing wildly, wracked with grief. It feels like my heart is breaking all over again, but this time, it's for the terrible truth in Sebastian's words.

He never loved you...

Suddenly, there's a commotion, and men in uniform swarm around. "Sebastian Wolfe?" the lead guy snaps, grabbing him roughly. It's Interpol, and they're right on time. I watch numbly as they read him his rights, and then take him away in handcuffs; I tipped them off ahead of time. Another piece of my plan.

The crowd watches him go, hushed in shock—and delight. I can see the gossip spreading, through all the important guests, as they revel in Sebastian's very public downfall. This will be front-page news for days.

But not everyone is celebrating.

"Seb?" there's a plaintive wail as he's led out. It's Bianca, looking devastated; Violetta barely holding her back. "Seb, tell me it's a lie. You didn't do this. You didn't kill my father!"

Sebastian keeps his head down; he doesn't say a word. And as they exit the garden, Bianca lets out a wretched sob of betrayal, practically sinking to the ground.

I should feel guilty. I should feel triumph. I should feel anything at all, seeing my plan work so perfectly.

But I can't feel anything at all.

Chapter 20

Avery

The party breaks up pretty soon after that. I guess there's nothing like the groom-to-be getting arrested to put a dampener on the party vibe.

I find myself wandering through the party wreckage, drinking straight from an open bottle of champagne. The staff have pretty much all scattered, and the guests are long gone. I'm the only one left to sample the exquisite chocolates, and the handmade cake with our names written in perfect script.

I try a bite, then push it aside. I can't stomach the rich flavor —or anything right now. So much for a celebration. I thought I'd be happy, finally getting my revenge.

Instead, I'm empty inside. Trying to ignore the whispers of doubt in the back of my mind.

He deserved this, I repeat to myself, heading back inside. *You did the right thing.*

The only thing.

I find my phone, and call Nero.

"It's done," I say as soon as he answers the phone. "Sebastian Wolfe is ruined."

"I saw," Nero replies. "It's headline news around the world. A powerful man like Sebastian, confessing to causing two deaths. Cable news is eating it up. Congratulations. You must be thrilled."

I must be.

"Yup, it's amazing," I lie, trying to sound enthusiastic. "It all played out exactly as I planned. Interpol came to arrest him, right after the article went live. Everyone saw him getting led away in handcuffs."

Nero chuckles. "I wish I could have been there to see it."

"I'm sure the footage will be online, soon enough. People had their cellphones out, filming. As a souvenir," I add bitterly.

"So if you're all wrapped up there, when can we expect you home?" Nero asks.

I pause. "I don't know," I reply slowly. To be honest, I'm not sure where home is anymore. I grew up in New York, with the Barretti family as my own, but with Nero moving on from the family business, starting a new, legit life with Lily, what place do I have there anymore?

A movement behind me makes me whirl around, and I find Richard strolling through the party décor with his trademark smarmy grin on his face. "I'll talk to you later," I tell Nero hurriedly. "I have to go."

I hang up and take a deep breath. "I thought everyone had left by now," I tell Richard, trying to get my game face on.

"I couldn't leave without offering you my congratulations." He says, smiling. "I knew you were a resourceful young lady, but I never imagined *this*."

"Thank you," I say coolly. "Now, if you don't mind, I have to deal with a few things."

"No time for a celebratory toast?" Richard asks. "I do so appreciate you doing what I couldn't and exposing him for the true villain he is. Honestly, I never would have guessed you had it in you. How did you know he was driving that night?"

I give a shrug. I've nothing to hide anymore.

"I tracked down the detective that investigated the accident, Officer Hardcastle," I tell him. "The story about what happened just didn't add up. And you can cut the bullshit innocent act with me," I add, challenging him directly. "You were the one paying everyone off to bury it. Sebastian was too young, he didn't have access to that kind of influence or money. But you did. You knew about this all along and covered his tracks. Why?"

Richard gives a sigh. "What else could I do? Trudy was devastated. The family had already lost so much. Subjecting them to a media circus, seeing Sebastian on trial... It would have been too much for her. I thought my nephew had made a tragic mistake, I had to protect them. They are my family, too, after all."

I narrow my eyes. I'm not buying it, but it's not my problem anymore.

"I had no idea Sebastian would grow up into a man like this," Richard continues, still acting like he's on some morning show. "But now, finally, he'll see the justice he's escaped for so long. Thanks to you, my dear."

"My pleasure," I reply dryly.

"So, what will you do now?" Richard asks.

I let out a hollow laugh. That's the question, isn't it?

"I'm not sure," I reply, looking out over the dark lake with a sigh. "I don't even know how I'm getting home from here, or where home even is anymore. I guess I didn't plan far enough ahead."

"You can take the jet back," Richard offers immediately. "It belongs to the company, and I'll be running Wolfe Capital now.

And of course, we own a number of apartments in London you can use. Until you figure things out."

I pause. I don't trust him, and I'm pretty sure these oh-so-generous offers will have strings attached.

Richard sees my hesitation. "You needn't worry," he says with a smirk. "It's a bargain, in my books. Since you've dealt with my nephew and offered up Wolfe Capital on a platter to me. I have no further business with you."

Slowly, I exhale. It's late, and I'm exhausted. I don't want to spend another moment here—surrounded by the happy memories I shared with Sebastian on our last trip to the house.

"Then, thank you," I decide. "I will use the flight. Can I leave tonight?"

"Of course, I'll call the airfield now," Richard says immediately. "Trudy is recovering back at our hotel, she's in quite a state, as you can imagine, having everything dredged up again. We'll probably stay a couple of days more, until she can travel. You'll have the plane to yourself."

Good.

I change into comfortable travel clothing and pack up my stuff while Richard calls the pilot and arranges a car to take me to the airport. I feel like I'm in a daze as I speed away from the villa, the dark countryside blurring outside the windows.

Was it worth it?

I replay the look in Sebastian's eyes when he realized I'd betrayed him. And the terrible things he said to me, those awful words about Miles...

"*You're foolish and naïve... That picture you've conjured of Miles is a lie... He never loved you... He left you all alone...*"

I shake my head, fighting the grief that's rising in my chest all over again. Sebastian was just lashing out. Trying to wound me.

I did the right thing.

I take off the engagement ring and slip it into my pocket as we arrive at the airfield. The car drives directly onto the tarmac, over to where Sebastian's small private jet is waiting by the hanger.

The driver brings my bags up the steps and into the cabin, and I follow, looking around. It's a small, luxuriously appointed space, with seats for ten people. But tonight, I'm the only passenger.

"Thank you, that will be all," I tell him, and tip him generously.

"*Buona notte*," he replies, and exits, leaving me alone.

I get settled into one of the comfortable reclining seats and snack on some grapes that were left out for me, hoping we can quickly get in the air. The adrenaline that has carried me through the past week is rapidly fading, leaving a bone-deep weariness in my limbs. The first thing I'll do when I get back to London is take a bath—and then sleep for a week.

I wait a while, expecting Sebastian's usual attendant to join me, but there's no one around. I hear movement in the cockpit, so I call out. "Hello?"

Suddenly, there's a clicking sound over the PA. The captain speaks, his voice muffled and crackly. "Apologies, but our usual attendant called in sick. It was such a last-minute call. But it will be a short flight, if you can manage alone."

"Of course," I call back. "Please, let's just go."

"Very well."

The engine starts, and I buckle my seatbelt, preparing to fly. We taxi away from the terminal, and I gaze out of the window, watching the scenery go by as the plane moves down the runway, gathering speed. It's a beautiful part of the world, and I wonder if I'll ever return, even as I know in my heart I could never come back here.

There are too many memories of Sebastian, and everything we shared.

The plane takes off smoothly, and soon enough, we're at cruising altitude. I stretch, yawning, and prepare to settle in for a nap, when suddenly, the door to the cockpit opens, and my pilot emerges.

Except, it's not the pilot.

It's Sebastian.

Terror strikes through me.

Oh God.

I look around for escape. But of course, there is none. We're trapped together, alone at twenty thousand feet.

"Hello, Sparrow," he drawls, eyeing me with an icy glare. "Enjoying the flight?"

"What's going on?" I gasp. "Where's the pilot? What did you do with him?"

"There is no pilot," Sebastian replies. His voice is ice cold and there's an ominous, dark look in his eyes. "It's just me and you up here, darling, and we're taking a little detour."

"A detour..." I glance out of the cabin window, and see nothing but snow and mountains below us.

"To my place in the Alps." Sebastian says, his gaze raking over me. "I thought we could use the quality time together. You see... The two of us are going to have a little chat."

"B-but what about the police?" I blurt, my mind racing. Sebastian was a dangerous man at the best of times, but now...?

Now I have no idea what he'll do to me.

Sebastian snorts with derision. "Did you really think they could hold me? I have the best lawyers around."

"They just let you go?" I can't believe it. This wasn't the plan.

"The accident was years ago, in England," Sebastian replies, settling into the leather seat opposite from me. "Besides, there's no proof linking me to the crash."

"What about the confession?" I demand.

He smirks. "You mean, the recording you made, illegally, without my consent? It'll never hold up in court."

My heart sinks. I can't believe he's escaped justice so easily. I can't believe I thought I had the better of him.

Sebastian leans closer. Like a predator eying his prey. "Avery Carmichael..." he murmurs it softly. "You were playing me from the start, weren't you? That poker game, the innocent act... It was all part of your plan. To win my trust, for a chance to have your revenge."

I think fast for some excuse, some lie to cover my tracks, but we're long past the lying now.

I raise my chin and meet his gaze, defiant.

"Yes," I answer. "It was all pretend. I never even liked you. I faked everything."

Sebastian chuckles dangerously. "Oh, but not *everything*. I know how you taste, darling. Remember? How your sweet cunt feels clenching on my cock, the way your eyes roll back when I made you my little whore. You couldn't fake that."

"But I hated myself for it," I vow angrily. "Every moment you were touching me, I wished I didn't feel a thing."

"Well, that makes two of us now, doesn't it?" Sebastian replies, reaching out to grip my jaw. "And if you thought you'd seen me angry before—"

BOOM!

A deafening explosion suddenly tears through the plane, sending us both sprawling to the floor. *Oh my god!* The plane dips, dangerously lurching, and to my horror, I see flames out of one window, the right wing crumpled and going up in smoke.

"Sebastian!" I scream, clawing to hold on to a seat as

freezing cold air rushes into the cabin, and the whole plane shaking and tossing around like it's made of paper.

"Hold on!" he yells, covering me with his body, protecting me as the plane shakes and dips. He pulls me towards the cockpit. I struggle after him, terror whirling in my chest.

"What do we do?" I cry, panicking.

He stumbles back into the pilot's seat. His movements are frantic as he pushes buttons and checks the instruments. "I can't get control. We're going down!"

Oh my God.

"Sit down and buckle up!" Sebastian yells at me, as he takes a hold of the yoke and yanks it violently. "We're going to have to emergency landing!"

I do what he says, fumbling with the belt in panic. I can see the dark mountains rearing up ahead of us, the snowy forests barely lit by our flashes of light. They're coming too fast. Too close.

"Sebastian!" I scream again, as we plow into the forest, the sound of crunching glass and metal deafening as the crushing impact sends me reeling.

And everything goes black.

To be continued...

What happens next? Avery and Sebastian's twisted love story comes to a shocking conclusion in Priceless Fate – available now!

PRICELESS: BOOK THREE
PRICELESS FATE

Vengeance is priceless...

They say when a man embarks on revenge, he should dig two graves.

But what about a woman?

I swore I'd destroy Sebastian Wolfe, no matter the cost. I surrendered my innocence - and my heart. But now, his secrets could be both our undoing.

Is he the monster I've been chasing?

Or the only man who can save me?

Discover the explosive final installment of the spicy, thrilling new saga from USA Today bestselling author Roxy Sloane, perfect for fans of Fifty Shades, Sierra Simone, and Sophie Lark.

THE PRICELESS SERIES:

Roxy Sloane is a USA Today bestselling author, with over 2 million books sold world-wide. She loves writing page-turning spicy romance full of captivatingly alpha heroes, sensual passion, and a sprinkle of glamor. She lives in Los Angeles, and enjoys shocking whoever looks at her laptop screen when she writes in local coffee shops.

* * *

To get free books, news and more, sign up to my VIP list!

www.roxysloane.com
roxy@roxysloane.com

Printed in Great Britain
by Amazon

36304391R00117